Józef Borusawski, S. Freeman

The Memoirs of the Celebrated Dwarf Joseph Boruwlaski

a Polish gentleman

Józef Borusawski, S. Freeman

The Memoirs of the Celebrated Dwarf Joseph Boruwlaski
a Polish gentleman

ISBN/EAN: 9783337287535

Printed in Europe, USA, Canada, Australia, Japan

Cover: Foto ©Andreas Hilbeck / pixelio.de

More available books at **www.hansebooks.com**

A SECOND EDITION OF

THE MEMOIRS

OF THE

Celebrated Dwarf,

JOSEPH BORUWLAS

A POLISH GENTLEMAN.

Containing

A faithful and curious Account

OF

HIS BIRTH, EDUCATION, MARRIAGE, T
AND VOYAGES.

WRITTEN BY HIMSELF; AND CARE
REVISED AND CORRECTED.

And translated from the French by Mr. S. F

Birmingham.

PRINTED BY J. THOMPSON.

1792.

SUBSCRIBERS.

Birmingham.

MR. J. Biffet, 2 copies
S. Toy
S. Vallant
J. Haffelden, 2 copies
J. Beddoes, prefident of the So-
ciety for Free Debate
Jofeph Smith
Samuel Smith
Timothy Smith
Robert Smith
John Miles
Jofeph Fearon, Conftable
James Murray
Thomas Pardoe
William Hallet
William Muchal
Michael Beafley
John Lowe, High-ftreet
William Steen
Jofeph Blunt
Edward Eagle
Benjamin Parkes
Richard Webfter
Robert Blyth
Thomas Small

Mr. J. Ofborn
S. Timmins
Benjamin Parker
John Lowe, 4 copies
J. Gill, New-ftreet
A. Afhmore
T. Akerman
A. Forreft
J. Collard
S. Ryland, *fenior*
Capt. D. Rufton
Mr. John Blount
T. Richards
A. C. Lageman
Peter Brown
John Merideth
—— Twamley
—— Linwood
Mifs Hunt
Mr. P. Price
Gaultier
J. Hawkins
King
R. B. Morgan
Richard Dingley
T. Blakemore
W. Collins
J. Ellis
W. Archer
W. Mills
R. Walford
J. Cox.
James Bedford
Edward Bedford
James Davies
Mark Sanders

Mr. John Moore
    J. Haywood
    John Freeth
    R. Hancock
    Thomas Clarke
    Joseph Taylor
    Thomas Bell
    Thomas Wilcox
    Roger Auster
    Henry Dixon
    R. S. Skey
    T. Parkes
    T. Phipson
    John Cope
    —— Cockle
    —— Shipton, 2 copies
    T. Richards, Gunsmith,
    Theophilus Richards
    Isaac Pratt
    John Kenrick
    Thomas Phillips
    —— Deeton
    —— Law
    John Barr
    —— Wright
    William Tabberner
    J. Thompson, Printer, 6 copies

Hereford.

Miss Oliva Lamb
Capt. Hatton
Miss Wilson
    Eurnell
    Stepurnell
Rev. Mr. Clark
Mr. Rash

Mr. James Wathen
  Francis Baladon Thomas
Mrs. Thomas
  Walwyn
  Phelps
  Terry
Mr. Hayward
Mrs. Hayward
Mr. Lambe
Doctor Blunt
Mrs. Blunt
Miss Benington
Mrs. Griffiths
Miss Griffiths
Mrs. Lucy
Mrs. Woodhouse
Mr. Joseph Thomas
Mr. William Thomas
Mr. T. Cotes
Rev. Mr. Core
Mr. George Terry
Mr. Brewster
Rev. Mr. Pope
Rev. Mr. Ronderwood
Miss A. Williams, Brecon
Mr. William Wathen

Gloucester.

Miss Harriot Saunders
Mrs. Foulks
Thomas Reynolds, Esq.
Mr. John Cook
Mr. Fox, Attorney
Sir John Guise
Mrs. Hayward

Mrs. Raikes
Mrs. Nicholls
Mrs. Ready
Mrs. Randall
Mrs. Saunders
Capt. Trigger
Rev. Joseph Cheston
Thomas Mee, Esq.
Charles Hayward, Esq. Quodgley
Rev. Samuel Commetine, Norton-House
John Wintle, *junior*, Esq. Nounham
David Arthur Saunders
Thomas Davies
T. Terry, Bookseller

Worcester.

Miss Saunders
Mr. Berwick
Mrs. Berwick
Mr. Letchmere
Mrs. Letchmere
Mr. ·················
Mr. ·················
Mr. ·················
Mr. ·················
William Hall, Esq. Beverre, near
    Worcester

Coventry.

Mr. Rollason
Mrs. Yardley, High-street
Mrs. Surinfin of Leicester

Shrewsbury.

Miss S. Loxdale
Lord de Montalt

Honourable Mr. Maude
Miſs Adelaide Congreve
Miſs Foreſter
Mr. Harnage
Miſs B. Foreſter
Miſs Owen
Mr. G. Dana
Miſs Floyd, St John's Hill
Mr. Dana
William Smith, Eſq.
Honourable Mrs. Dana
Miſs Bingham
Miſs Loxdale
Mr. Sulton, Surgeon
Miſs B. Smitheman
Mr. W. Anwil
Rev. Edward Kynaſton
Mr. Betton
Mr. Geary
Mr. Podmore
Mr. Thomas Vaughan
Miſs Edwards
Mr. Hollings
Mr. Cludde
R. de Courcy
Miſs Margaret Adams
Mr. Edwards
Rev. Mr. Lloyd
Mr. Bage
Mrs. Adams
Mr. Ottley
Miſs Raiſtford
Thomas Dowdeſwell, Eſq.
Richard Murrhall, Eſq.
Miſs E. Adams
John Lacy

Mr. Wingfield, The Hall
Mr. J. Gate
Mr. W. Ferriday
Mr. Mafon
Mifs Heighway
Mr. J. Stedman
Mifs C. Rainsford
Mr. S. Sandford
Mr. Eddowes
Mrs. Inge
Dr. Darwin
Mrs. Hodges
Mrs W. Coupland
Mifs Owen
Mr. J. Loxdale.

Bridgnorth.

Mifs M. Dethick
Geo. Boulton
Benjamin Watts
Rev. Thomas Dethick
James Marfhall
Mrs. Dethick
Rev. Mr. Blyth
Mrs. Allan
Mrs. Petty
Mrs. Blyth
Mrs. Lampit
Mrs. Gatcare
Rev. W. Ellifon
G. Gitton
Mifs Smith
Mifs Devey
Mr. J. A. Burney
Mrs. Congreve
Rev. Mr. Feutrell

Thomas Barnfield
Rev. M. Atterood, Bifherby
F. Williams
Rev. Thomas Lyfter
Mifs Rhodes
Mrs. Braithwaite

....

Mifs Snead, *Ludlow*
Rev. Mr. Snead, *ditto*
Mifs Ann Miere, *ditto*
Mifs Cottrell, *ditto*
Rev. Mr. Wellings, *ditto*
Mrs. Foldervey, *ditto*
Dr. Mofeley, *ditto*
Mr. Jofeph Miere, Berington,
Mr. Whitfield, Surgeon at Wenlock
M. Du Longprey, Cherburg
Mr. Charles Mollen, Guernfey
Mr. Metivier, *ditto*
Mr. Guiles de St George
Sir Robert Goodere, Margaret-ftreet,
    Cavendifh-fquare, London.
Mifs J. Vernon, Welbeck-ftreet, *ditto*
Capt. Baker, No. 4, Wimpole-ftreet, *ditto*
Mrs. V. Corbet, Welbeck-ftreet, *ditto*
Peregrine Deattry, Efq. Berkley-ftreet,
    Manchefter-fquare, *ditto*
Captain Wells, G. Rogers, Efq. Spring-
    Gardens, *ditto*
Captain Baker, Parliament-ftreet, *ditto*
Thomas Anfon, Efq. St James's fquare
Francis Glanville, Efq. Lower Berkley-
    Street, Portman-fquare, *ditto*
Mrs. Adair, Pall-mall, *ditto*
Mifs Afhmall, Eaft-ftreet, Red-Lion-
    fquare, *ditto*

Sir Thomas Fleetwood, Bart. No. 58, Gower-
ftreet, Bedford-fquare, London
Lady Fleetwood   [Oxford,
Rev. Charles Neve, B. D. St. John's College,
Rev. Henry Harrifon, B. D. Northampton
Mr. Samuel Statham, Nottingham
Mrs. Froft, *ditto*
Mrs. Gawthern, *ditto*
Mrs. Roe, Fletcher-gate, *ditto*
Thomas Dufty, Market-place, *ditto*
Mr. Amys, *ditto*
Mr. Allen, *ditto*
Simeon Moreau, Efq. M. C. Cheltenham,
Rev. Dr. Small, Briftol
Rev. Dr. White, Gloucefter
———— Surinfen, Efq. near Lichfield,
———— Repington, Efq. *ditto*
Drewry Ottlew, Efq. Teddington   ·   [folk
Thomas Gurdon, Efq. Letton, Thetford, Nor-
Mrs. Prattinton, Bewdley, Worcefterfhire
Mrs. Berington
John Dela Bere, Efq. Efq. Cheltenham
Lt. Col. M'Clary, Speenhill, Berks
Mr. Buckle, Myth, near Tewkefbury
Sir William Altham, near Leatherhead, Surrey
Thomas Reynolds, Efq. Briftol,
Mrs. Douglas, Teddrington
Earl of Dumfries, Ecoffe
Rev. Mr. Clutton, Hereford
Mifs Calcot, Berwick, near Shrewfbury
Mr. Sandford, Wellington, *ditto*
Edward Gatacre, Efq. Gatacre,
John Hale, Efq. Hollies,
Mr. Plowden, Prefland,
Mr. Robert Britton, Sheffield
Mifs Horfley, Henley in Arden
Mr. James, *fenior, ditto*

Mr. Barber, *ditto*
Mr. Richard Reeve, Henley in Arden
Mr. Lea, Attorney, *ditto*
Rev. Mr. Chambers, Studley, 2 copies
Mr. Batteſon, Birmingham, 2 copies
Geo. Banniſter, Eſq. Salter-ſtreet
Richard Field, Eſq. Blackford
Capt. Hunt, Tanworth
Mr. Morris, Stratford on Avon
    J. Brookehouſe, Bromſgrove
    J. Connard, *ditto*
    W. Turton, Dudley
    S: Nock, *ditto*
    Peter Walker, *ditto*
    John Eagle, *ditto*
    Hickman, *ditto*
    R. Parſons, *ditto*
    W: Fellows, *ditto*
    G. R. Shaw, *ditto*
    E. Derby, Rowley
    Brandon Whiſſel, Alceſter
    Somerville, of Hinkley
    Haſſel, Solyhull
    Weſton, *ditto*
    Patteſon, Smethwick
    W. Smith, Dunnington-mill,
    J. Davies, London
    T. Liddiard, *ditto*
    W. Brooke, *ditto*
    D. F. Noon, *ditto*
    J. Fayner, Liverpool,
    Kempſon, Cleobury-Mortimer,
    Chambers, Stourbridge
    James Jacks, Charleſtown, South Carolina
    Geo. Schepler, *ditto*
    A. Biſſet, Edinburgh
    St. John's Lodge, Henley in Arden, 10 copies

TO HER GRACE

The Duchefs of Devonfhire,

MADAM,

NO words can exprefs the obligations I am under, not only for your unremitted favours conferred upon me from the very moment of my arrival in England, but alfo for the completion of them by your condefcenfion, in permitting me to dedicate to your Grace thefe Memoirs, and thereby attempt, however feebly, to manifeft my gratitude. On their reception in the world, entirely depends my future welfare, and my family's fupport. Can I entertain the leaft doubt of their meeting with a general ac-acceptance, when they are prefented under your

Grace's

Grace's auspices and patronage? How flattering is the idea, how delightful is the prospect,
to be indebted for all to a protectress, who, still
more by her talents and internal qualities, than
by the charms of external elegance, victoriously
sways every heart.....But here I stop.....Though
my feelings may be ever so lively, yet they cannot impart the talents which are wanting in
me, and considering my inherent insufficiency, I
must only admire in silence.

I am, with the most profound respect,

MADAM,

Your GRACE'S

Most obedient

Most dutiful and

Humble Servant,

(S

JOS. BORUWLASKI.

PREFACE.

THE person whom these Memoirs presents us the history of, cannot fail of being interesting. 'Tis not one of those mis-shapen beings whom nature seems to have barely conceived, and which, in fact, either by its deficiency in physical effects, or by the privation of intellectual powers, holds to our view a degrading object, which humanity recoils at:—No; Joseph Boruwlaski, favoured by nature, possesses every qualification which constitutes a man; dis-

tinctly

tinctly organized, healthful, well-made, only differing in fize. It is this which renders him worthy of admiration. Thus, when we behold a fmall watch, we juftly admire it as a mafter-piece of workmanfhip, when, notwithftanding its diminutive appearance, we percieve it marks the hours, &c. with precifion and regularity.

From his earlieft youth, Jofeph Boruwlafki's fame was fpread : It was not the public curiofity alone he excited, he drew the attention of the literati; kings and emperors, with the firft nobility of different kingdoms, empires, and ftates, and the moft illuftrious of the fair fex, honoured him with their attention; as thefe Memoirs will fufficiently authenticate.

The

The better to afcertain the confidence of our readers, as to the facts
herein related, we beg leave to remind
them of an anecdote wrote and print-
ed in the Encyclopedia, about thirty
years fince, in the article *Dwarf*, both
as it refers to J. B. and to another
dwarf belonging to King Staniflaus,
and well known by the name of Bébé.
There is the following relation of
him: " I begin with the Dwarf of
his Majefty the King of Poland, Duke
of Lorraine. He was the eldeft of
three children; was called Nicholas
Ferry; born the 19th of September,
1741; his mother at that time thirty-
five years old. Notwithftanding the
ufual fymptoms of pregnancy declared
themfelves before this child's birth,
his mother would not be perfuaded
fhe was with child, till fhe had fuffer-

ed

ed the pains of childbirth for forty-eight hours. He was, at his birth, nine inches long, and weighed about fifteen ounces; a common fhoe, half full of wool, ferved him for a cradle for fome time; for he was the fon of a peafant, on the Vofgan Mountains.

The 25th of July, 1746, M. Kaft, Phyfician to the Queen Duchefs of Lorraine, meafured and weighed him with great attention; he weighed, when naked, nine pounds feven ounces; fince that time he grew to thirty-fix inches in height. He had the fmall-pox at three months old; his countenance was not difagreeable in his infancy, but much altered fince.

Bébé

Bébé, is the name that was given him at King Staniſlaus' court; Bébé, I ſay, who is now (in 1760) in his twentieth year, ſeems bent with age; his complexion withered, one ſhoulder higher than the other, his aquiline noſe now deformed; his mind never formed, nor could they ever learn him to read."

Another article inſerted in a Supplement to the Encyclopedia, gives the following account of the ſame: " Bébé had ever very imperfect conceptions; nor could they impreſs on him any idea of a Supreme Being, or of the immortality of the ſoul; which was fully proved in his laſt tedious ſickneſs, which proved mortal. He appeared fond of muſic, and would often beat time with preciſion; they even

ſucceeded

fucceeded fo far as to make him dance;
but when dancing, he had his eyes
fixed upon his dancing-mafter, who
by figns directed all his motions, as
we fee in feveral trained animals.
He was fufceptible of thofe paffions
common to brutes; fuch as anger and
jealoufy. He had however his faculties free, and, in regard to phyfio-
logy, appeared perfect, and according
to the courfe of nature. About feventeen or eighteen years of age evident
figns of manhood appeared, and even
vigorous for his fize: it feems fufficiently proved that his duenna had
for a long time mifufed it; and Bébé's
fudden infirmities were thought the
confequence of imprudent exceffes.

By all the obfervations I could
poffibly make upon the organifm of
this

this little being, I particularly re-
marked, that he died of old age before
he was thirty; for indeed at twenty-
two he was in a kind of dotage; and
thofe who had the care of him thought
they could diftinguifh a fecond child-
hood, that is to fay, an increafe of
dotage.

The laft year of his life, he could
fcarce fupport himfelf; he feemed
worn down with age. He could not
bear the open air; but, in a warm
day they made him walk in the fun-
fhine, and he could then fcarce fupport himfelf as he walked.

This was his epitaph :—Here lies
Nicholas Ferry, Lorraine, the fport
of nature, wonderful in the fmallnefs
of his ftructure, cherifhed by the
New

new Antonine, old in youth, five luftres were to him an age; he died June 9, 1761.

You will now fee what they fay concerning Jofeph Boruwlafki*, Madam Humiefka's dwarf, named M. Boruwlafki, a Polonefe gentleman, is far different from that of King Staniflaus, and this young gentleman muft be admired as a phænomenon of nature.

He is now (1760) 22 years of age, 28 inches high, and perfectly well-fhaped, his head in proportion, his eyes penetrating, his knees, legs, and feet, well proportioned; and we are

---

* M. Boruwlafki did not belong to Madame Humiefka, as you will fee in this hiftory; he was on a quite different footing, and a companion in her travels.

assured

affured his manhood indubitable; his drink water, eats little, fleeps well, fupports fatigue, and enjoys perfect health.

He unites wit and good fenfe to a graceful deportment, a good memory, and found judgment, a tender heart and formed for friendfhip and love.

Mr. Boruwlafki's parents were above the common fize, and of a good conftitution. They have fix children; the eldeft thirty-four inches, well made; the fecond Jofeph, (of whom we now fpeak), only twenty-eight inches; three younger brothers, yearly fucceffive to each other, were about five feet fix inches, and robuft, and well fhaped; the fixth and laft child was a daughter, now fix years old,

old, from twenty to twenty-one inches, elegantly fhaped, and beautiful features, her geftures and fpeech fimilar to thofe of her age, and a rival of her fecond brother in wit and gracefulnefs.

Mr. J. Boruwlafki remained a long time uncultivated. It is about two years fince that Mad. Humiefka educated him; he now is well verfed in arithmetic, fpeaks French and German, and promifes ftrength of genius in every thing he undertakes.

The Reader muft, on perufal of thefe articles, be thoroughly convinced of the vifible difference eftablifhed by nature in the fame fpecies; how varioufly ftamped; what a contraft between the unfortunate Bébé and the

truly

truly amiable Boruwlaſki. The effects of Nature's partiality is viſibly
productive; for while we behold Bébé
leading a paſſive and indolent life,
nay, we may ſay, inanimate, border-
ing on ſtupidity, in Staniſlaus' court,
—we view with pleaſure Joſeph Boruwlaſki, by poſſeſſing enlivening faculties, and mature judgment, graceful manners, energy and ſenſibility,
on a level with the reſt of mankind,—
we behold him with admiration travelling through different ſtates of
Europe, croſſing ſeas, overbounding
mountains, deſpiſing dangers, exer-
ciſing both phyſical and moral exiſtence,—reſiſting the fatigues inſepar-
able from long journies, the incle-
mency of ſeaſons, and variation of
climates, manners and cuſtoms, change
of food and manner of living; ſucceeding

ceeding every where, beloved every where, univerſally attracting not formal and ceremonious greetings, but anxious, tender, and unlimitted endeavours to promote his happineſs; when, on himſelf depending, boldly exerting himſelf, expoſed to the viciſſitudes of fortune, nothing diſcouraged; ſtruggling with fortune, he commands her—He is (if we may be permitted the expreſſion) all Soul: we may juſtly compare him to thoſe little phials filled with eſſence. Boruwlaſki's pecuniary circumſtances correſpond not with his merits. Father of a numerous family, he candidly acknowledges his ſituation, and why ſhould he bluſh to confeſs it? Is he apprehenſive of being forſaken? No; he is too well convinced of the benevolence of the age. Nature has not de-

voted

voted him forlorn; she has marked him a favourite; she has been a kind mother, and conducted him to perfection; she has not contracted him, like many of the same species; Bébé died at twenty-five years of age, infirm, old, and decrepid; similar deaths of two other dwarfs are mentioned in a philosophical treatise, who at fifteen years of age had every appearance of caducity, and whom nature seemed to have formed for curiosity alone, and prudently withdrew them from the world, at that fatal crisis when no longer objects of curiosity, they could only remain a burthen to society, despised and neglected by her : but this same nature has prolonged the life of Joseph Boruwlaski, because she had formed him for far more noble views than mere curiosity, curiofity,--- he was deftined to fet forth her unlimitted powers---formed to attract at once the contemplative mind, and elevated foul.

In fact, how many claims to her favour! Bleft with a virtuous and amiable wife *, father of four children, the eldeft only eleven years of age, himfelf attained his fifty-third year, deprived of no one faculty, his intellects replete, he appears deftined to a good old age; fhall he then fear to be forfaken when his wants increafe? No; forbid it humanity: no; vanifh the thought; an enlightened nation, in whofe bofom he has fought an afylum, will never abandon his

* His wifeois of a middling ftature, and the children proportioned.

little

little exiſtence ſo truly wonderful to ſhame and contempt; whoſe exiſtence, whether moral or phyſical, forms the greateſt phænomenon nature has ever produced.

In regard to this hiſtory which we preſent to the public, wrote by M. Boruwlaſki himſelf, it was print-ed and ſold in 1788, and with great ſuccefs. Mr. Boruwlaſki, folicited by ſeveral perfons in the kingdom, has thought fit to publiſh a new edition, hoping to entertain many of his readers, he has made ſome flight alte-rations, particularly as in the former he had ſuppreſſed many intereſting faſts; viſits paid or received by the author, and the favourable receptions he met with. It was with great dif-

ficulty

ficulty M. Boruwlaſki was perſuaded
to make theſe omiſſions, not with the
view that the homage he paid to the
ſeveral perſons ſignified might prove
beneficial to him, who are all of note
in England, but becauſe this homage
appeared to him a teſtimony of his
gratitude, and, as he ſaid, this motive
of his delicacy ought alone to forbid
him.

We moreover think this hiſtory
worthy of intereſting the upright
mind, who only requires of any object what it is capable of.

The facts pointed out in this hiſtory are by no means important:
they are in no wiſe connected with
the great events of Europe, which ſo
ſtrongly

ftrongly imprefs all nations; they
bear a proportion to the object de-
fcribed; they are in a manner cor-
refpondent to his fize : but extent is
not the firft requifite of works of this
nature; the pine-apple is more deli-
cious than the gourd; the humble re-
feda fpreads forth a perfume which never graced the lofty chefnut:—In the
eye of a philofopher no ftudy is con-
temptible, no object trivial in itfelf:
it is as from the leaves of a ftrawberry-
plant, that the author, from the ftu-
dies of Nature, has fhot forth into the
univerfal fyftem. The little being we
now fpeak of, might eafily lead us to
reflections as immenfe : but in giving
his hiftory, we only mean to fix the
public attention on his perfon. We
fhall only add, that the facts herein

ɔ   mentioned

mentioned are indubitable, and have never been called in queſtion by the numerous and reſpectable witneſſes now living.

MEMOIRS.

ERRATA.

Page 13, line 6, for *Paradice* read *Paradise*.
70———13,   *who* read *whom*.
71——— 4,   *toe rnounce* read *to renounce.*
72———17,   *I know not* read *I knew not.*
———19,   *is dreadful* read *was dreadful*
80———21,   *heorine* read *heroine*
98———14,   *didsose* read *dispose*
120———16,   *desart* read *desert*
121——— 3,   *I am now bound* read *I proposed to go.*
122——— 9,   *d'Almazasyue* read *d'Almazague.*
124———18,   *Two thousand* read *twenty thousand.*
125———13,   *claims* read *claim.*

N. B. The Preface to these Memoirs was written by M. de St. Alphonse, of Paris.

MEMOIRS.

I T is fo uncommon to find reafon
and fentiment, with noble and delicate affections, in a man whom nature, as it were,
could not make up, and who in fize has the
appearance of a child, that, perfuaded nobody would even take the trouble to caft
an eye upon thefe Memoirs, I began to
commit to paper fome of the principal
events of my life, by way of memorandums,
for my own ufe, only to remind me of the
different fituations I had been in, to recal to

B   my

my memory fcenes too interefting, emotions too ftrong, to die in oblivion. As the reflections which I fhall have occafion to make can be interefting only to thofe who delight in following nature through all her different ways, who are wont to look upon beings of my ftature as upon abortive half-grown individuals, kept far beneath other men, both in body and mind; and who, confequently, may be curious to fee one of them affimilate himfelf to creatures of a common fize, as to his views, affections, paffions, and ideas; I fhould not have taken the liberty of prefenting them to the public, had not perfons to whom I ought not to refufe any thing, impofed it upon me as a duty. May I be fo happy, when I offer this tribute of my gratitude, as to convince them how deeply I felt the intereft they took in my concerns.

I was born in the environs of Chaliez, the capital of Pokucia, in Polifh Ruffia, in
November

November 1739. My parents were of the middle fize; they had fix children, five fons and one daughter; and by one of thofe freaks of nature which it is impoffible to account for, or perhaps to find another inftance of in the annals of the human fpecies, three of thefe children grew to above the middle ftature, whilft the two others, like myfelf, reached only that of children in general at the age of four or five years.

I am the third of this aftonifhing family. My eldeft brother, who at this time is above fixty, is near three inches taller than I am; he has conftantly enjoyed a robuft conftitution, and has ftill ftrength and vigour much above his fize and age; he has lived a long time with the Caftelane Inowlofka, who honours him with her efteem and bounty; and finding in him ability and fenfe enough, intrufts him with the ftewardfhip and management of her affairs.

My

My fecond brother was of a weak and delicate frame; he died at twenty-fix, being at that time five feet ten inches high. Thofe who came into the world after me, were alternately tall and fhort: among them was a fifter, who died of the fmall-pox at the age of twenty-two. She was at that time only two feet two inches high, and to a lovely figure united an admirably well proportioned fhape.

- It was eafy to judge from the very inftant of my birth, that I fhould be extremely fhort, being at that time only eight inches in length; yet, notwithftanding this diminutive proportion, I was neither weak nor puny: on the contrary, my mother, who fuckled me, has often declared that none of her children gave her lefs trouble. I walked, and was able to fpeak, at the age common to other infants, and my growth was progreffively as follows: ·

At

At one year I was 11 inches high, Englifh meafure, '

At three	—	1 foot 2 inches
At fix	——	1 - 5
At ten	——	1 - 9
At fifteen	—	2 feet 1
At twenty	—	2 - 4
At twenty-five		2 - 11
At thirty	—	3 - 3

This is the fize at which I remained fixed, without having afterwards increafed half a quarter of an inch. My brother, as well as myfelf, grew till thirty years of age, and at that period ceafed to grow. I cite this double proof to remove the opinion of fome naturalifts, who have advanced, that dwarfs continue to grow all their life.

I had fcarcely entered my ninth year when my father died, and left my mother with fix children, and a very fmall fhare in

the

the favours of fortune: a circumſtance to
which I am indebted for the part I have
ſince acted in the world. Had it not been
ſo, I ſhould undoubtedly have paſſed my days
in a province on the banks of the Nieſter,
where I might have experienced more happineſs.

A friend of my mother, the Staroſtina
de Caorliz, ſhewed me much affection, and
often had ſolicited my parents to commit
my education to her care. She availed herſelf of the embarraſſed circumſtances of our
family, to repeat her kind offers to my mother, who, though it might prove grievous
to her, yielded to the deſire of making me
happy; and inſiſting no longer on keep-
ing me at home, conſented, but not without tears, to part with me; and Lady de
Caorliz took me to her eſtate, which was
not far from my mother's abode.

We

We had no fooner arrived there, than the Staroftina, eager to fulfil her promifes to my mother, beftowed upon me all the care that my age required. I lived with her four years; and, the fondnefs of my bene-factrefs no way diminifhing, I was likely to be fixed for ever with her, when an unexpected event changed the face of things.

Lady de Caorliz was a widow, fomewhat advanced in years, but ftill blooming and graceful: befides, fhe enjoyed a large fortune. The Count de Tarnow, whom fome affairs had drawn to the neighbourhood, paid his court to her, and I foon perceived fhe highly diftinguifhed him above all the perfons who compofed her fociety. She became penfive and abfent; fhe feemed no longer amufed with my little prattling; and I was not furprifed at feeing Hymen unite thefe two lovers. Nor was I unconfcious of the alteration my fituation would fuffer by their marriage. I percieved that

my

my protectress, by taking a husband, had given herself a master, that, should I chance to displease him, I was in danger of being so much the more embarrassed, as my family affairs, which were totally overthrown, left me no resource; therefore I considered it as my duty to be more assiduous in my efforts, that I might render myself agreeable to the husband of my benefactress; and I think I should have succeeded, had not a new event disappointed me, and given rise to other projects.

Some months after their marriage, the Countess de Tarnow thought she was pregnant. The joy of this happy couple may be easily conceived. They were congratulated on this occasion by all their friends, among whom they reckoned the Countess Humieska. This lady, who was descended from one of the most ancient families in Poland, was held in the highest rank in that country, not more for her birth and wealth, than

than for her perfonal qualities. Her eftate
being fituated near the feat of the Staroftina,
fhe had frequent opportunities of feeing me,
and feemed to have fome affection for me, as
fhe often expreffed what pleafure fhe would
have if I came to live with her at Rychty.
My anfwers to her obliging offers gained me
her friendfhip more and more; nay, from that
moment, fhe had very likely formed the
project to afk me of the Countefs de Tarnow, and only waited for a favourable opportunity.

The pregnancy of my protectrefs furnifhed the Countefs Humiefka with a pretext. Being one day with the married pair,
fhe artfully infinuated that maternal love
would prevent the Countefs from fharing
her tendernefs with me, and the infant, when
born; and concluded, by offering to take
me home with her, promifing faithfully the
greateft care of my little perfon, and of my
future welfare.

Whether

Whether they doubted that the new object of their tenderness might impede their attention to my future education, or whether they were cautious of disobliging the Countess, they but weakly resisted, and declared they left it to my decision. I was absent: the servant who came to fetch me, informed me of what had passed. I entered the apartment, quite prepared with my answer, and assured the Countess, that, if the Lady de Tarnow, whose bounty rendered her the mistress of my fate, deigned to grant me her consent, I should deem myself happy to live under the protection of the Countess, and would follow my inclination as much as my duty, by earnestly endeavouring to deserve her kindness.

The Countess Humieska seemed overjoyed at my consent: I am very glad, said she, my dear Joujou (for so they called me), to see you have no reluctance to come and live with me. Then addressing the Count

Count and Countefs de Tarnow: You cannot retract, fhe faid; I have your word and
that of Joujou. The remainder of the vifit
paffed in compliments, and our departure
was fixed for a few days after.

Although I was under great obligations
to the Countefs de Tarnow, yet I own that I
was foon eafily reconciled to my feparation
from her. For this I hope I fhall be forgiven,
on confidering that I was but fifteen, having
my head filled with the lively picture my
protectrefs had given me of the pleafures I
fhould enjoy at her houfe. She carried me
to her eftate, at Rychty in Podolia, where
we ftayed fome time; and where fhe received
a vifit from a Pacha of Hocim, a Turkifh
city nigh Rychty. This Turkifh grandee,
not more eminent by his rank of Pacha,
than by his amiable, polite, and affable manners, invited my benefactrefs to vifit his
palace at Hocim. I was prefent at this
invitation, and heard with pleafure that he
politely

politely requested that I would accompany the Countess, declaring that the sight of a seraglio would afford me entertainment: I went with the Countess. On our arrival, we were received with all the honours due to the rank of my protectress; and, as for me, I was much delighted and caressed in the palace: for they were informed of our coming. We were served, amongst other entertainments, with an elegant collation after the Turkish manner: the sherbet was not spared. I was highly delighted with the expectation of being admitted into the seraglio, of which I had heard the Pacha speak; but I had no idea of it at that time; only having heard my benefactress say that they were grand apartments that contained many pretty things. How agreeably was I surprized, when I beheld about twenty beautiful women! all tender, affectionate, and polite in their caresses! With what pleasure do I reflect on the natural bloom of their complexions, the symmetry of their

features,

features, their chearful and modeſt deportment, their elegant ſhape, their enchanting
expreſſions, their majeſtic air, their graceful
behaviour!—In ſhort, it was here I beheld
beauty in perfection! For Mahomet's promiſed houries in Paradice are not more ac-
compliſhed. They were natives of Cir-
caſſia, and that country is univerſally allow-
ed to have ever produced paragons of
beauty, adorned with all the charms of the
Graces, far ſuperior to the other parts of
the world. I ſhall not enter into a particular deſcription of the ſeraglio, as it only
reſembles thoſe ſo often deſcribed by travellers, none of whom, in fact, have been
admitted like me, by ſpecial favour, within
the interior apartments; but the ſmallneſs
of my ſtature procured me this very particular honour.

Her Ladyſhip, whoſe deſign was to ſee
Germany and France, deſiring to have me
with her, I felt the greateſt pleaſure in the
flattering

flattering idea I entertained of thofe travels. After fome indifpenfible preparations, we fet out for Vienna.

The reader, perhaps, will not be dif-pleafed to know the manner of travelling in Poland. At that time I was too young, and my mind too little improved to be much impreffed with it; but it has hurt my feelings much fince upon reflection.

Let it be firft imagined, that on the roads there are neither inns or public-houfes of any kind to be found, nor any decent re-fort wherein the traveller can meet with the leaft conveniency; that confequently he is obliged to carry with him his kitchen fur-niture, houfehold goods, and provifions; that he fees nothing in the country he goes through, but fome difpicable villages, chiefly inhabited by Jews; that in the dwelling of thofe poor wretches, a kind of barn where men and animals live promifcuoufly toge-

ther,

ther, Polifh travellers take their abode; that they take care to fend before them fome fervants, who choofing the place they think moft convenient, drive the inhabitants out of it, often with heavy lafhes, and even ufe the fame violence fometimes upon other travellers, who, being inferior in rank, dare not contend for the fpot; that the fervants, being in poffeffion of the place, cover the walls with hangings, fet up beds and the furniture they have brought; fo that the mafters, when they arrive, find their lodgings ready and decently furnifhed. It may be eafily imagined, that fuch infolent fervants fpare not the poultry and vegetables of the poor Jews, who, whilft their property is thus difpofed of, feek for refuge in fome neighbouring hovels, wherein they impatiently wait for the departure of thofe troublefome guefts, that they may return to their own home again.

After fome days of very fatiguing travel, and a dull ftay for fome months at Leopold, we we reached Vienna; where the report of our arrival was no sooner spread, than we were visited, invited, and entertained with the utmost eagerness. Soon after we had the honour to be presented to her Imperial Majesty the Queen of Hungary; who was graciously pleased to say, that I exceeded by far all that she had heard of me, and that I was one of the most astonishing beings she had ever seen. At that time, this great Princess was engaged in war with the King of of Prussia, and, by her firmness, courage and wisdom, had rendered herself no less terrible to her enemies than dear to her subjects. I had the honour to be one day in her apartment, when her courtiers complimented her on a victory obtained by her army, and every one extolled the advantageous consequences of it, so that, according to their account, the King of Prussia was likely to be soon reduced to the last extremity.

The Empress, near whom I stood, asked me how the King of Prussia was looked

upon

upon in Poland? and what idea I entertained of that Prince? Madam, I anfwered, I have not the honour to know him; but were I in his place, inftead of lofing my time in waging an ufelefs war againft you, I would come to Vienna, and pay my refpects to you, deeming it a thoufand times more glorious to gain your efteem and friendfhip, than to obtain the moft complete victories over your troops. Her Imperial Majefty feemed much pleafed at my reply, clafped me in her arms, and faid to my benefactrefs, fhe efteemed her very happy in having fo pleafing a companion in her travels.

Another time, when, according to her defire, I had performed a Polifh dance in the prefence of this fovereign, fhe took me on her lap, and after having much careffed me, and afked many queftions how I fpent my time, fhe wifhed to know what I found at Vienna moft curious and interefting: I
anfwered,

anfwered, I had feen there many things worthy of a traveller's admiration, but nothing
feemed to me fo extraordinary as what I beheld at that moment.—And what is it?
faid her Majefty.—It is, replied I, to fee fo
little a man on the lap of fo great a woman.
This anfwer gained me new careffes. The
Emprefs had on her finger a ring, upon
which her cypher was fet in brilliants, with
the moft exquifite workmanfhip. My hand
being by chance locked in hers, I feemed to
look upon the ring attentively, which fhe
perceived, and afked whether that cypher
was pretty.—I beg your Majefty's pardon,
replied I, it is not the ring I admire, but
the hand, which I befeech you give me
leave to kifs; and with thefe words I took
it to my lips. The Emprefs feemed charmed
at this little gallantry, and would have prefented me with the ring which had caufed
it; but the circle proving too wide, fhe
called to a young princefs about five or
fix years old, who was then in the apartment,

ment, took from her finger a very fine diamond fhe wore, and put it on mine. This young Princefs is now the Queen of France; and it may be imagined I carefully preferve fo precious a jewel.

It is eafy to underftand, that the kind notice which the Emprefs honoured me with procured me the attention of the court; and I fhould be guilty of ingratitude, were I filent on the kindnefs his Excellency the Prince Kaunitz fhewed me. This great man, who at that time was ruling, as he ftill does, all the affairs of the German empire, could yet afford fome time to fpend on more trivial objects; and I may fay, that the marks of friendfhip and intereft he honoured me with would have raifed many jealoufies, had not my fize and mode of exiftence put me out of the common line. He, in a princely manner, offered me a genteel penfion for life; but my benefactrefs, fomewhat hurt, replied, that fhe had

fortune

fortune fufficient; and that being with her
was fufficient reafon for me to reject any
pecuniary offers.   He called me his little
friend, pretending that my converfation both
amufed and interefted him.   In a word, on
this journey, and on that I fhall fpeak of
hereafter, I had fo much reafon to be well
pleafed with his beneficence, that my only
regret is, not to have any other means of
teftifying to him how deeply my heart is
imprefsed with the remembrance of it.

Thofe, however, would be much mif-
taken, who fhould imagine that, feduced by
the repeated kindneffes beftowed on me, or
wholly devoted to the pleafures afforded
me, I did not fometimes labour under painful feelings, or that I could always be unconfcious of being, upon the whole, only
looked upon by others as a doll, a little more
perfect, it is true, and better organized than
they commonly are, but, however, only an
animated toy.   I remember, among other
things,

things, that one day, in the apartment of my benefactrefs, when fitting in a corner at a little diftance, and apparently paying no attention to their converfation, I heard they were fpeaking of me. One of the company having put the queftion, whether dwarfs poffefs the faculty of procreating? another advanced, that if they have it, their children would grow to the common fize; and the Countefs Humiefka acquainted her company with the ftate of my family, and in particular of my fifter, whofe fize, fhe faid, is ftill more extraordinary than that of Joujou. She added, fhe had often revolved in her own mind, how pleafant it would be to join thefe two little creatures, that the refult might decide the queftion. I fpare my readers the particulars of that converfation, which was carried very far, and only interrupted by my weeping bitterly; fo ftrongly was I affected at the fort of contempt apparently implied in this project of uniting me to my fifter; from which I thought I had

to

to conclude, not only that they believed themfelves entitled to difpofe of me without my advice, but even looked upon me as a being merely phyfical, without morality, on whom they might try experiments of every kind. Somebody in the company perceiving my grief, wifhed to know the caufe of it, which I perfifted in concealing; and at length, not being able to ftand againft the folicitations of my benefactrefs, I declared it to her, who had much ado to confole me, though fhe affured me fhe had never ferioufly thought on a marriage, of which the idea alone had fhocked me fo much. After all, I only relate this event to. fhow, that though ftill very young, during my firft ftay at Vienna, yet I was fo far improved, and had acquired fo much experience, as to feel all the impreffions natural to thofe of my age.

We ftayed at Vienna fix months only, during which time my benefactrefs, availing
herfelf

C

herfelf of the opportunity, had me taugl es dancing by Mr. Angelini, the ballet-mafte. to the Court, who fince, by his eminent talents in his art, and his tafte for literature, has rendered himfelf fo famous. Unluckily for me, being obliged to depart, I could not improve under his care as much as I wifhed : yet my benefactrefs could not forbear teftifying with raptures, at what fhe called my progrefs, her gratitude to him, at our fetting off from Bavaria.

Arriving at Munich, we were moft gracioufly welcomed by his Electoral Highnefs, and it feemed I excited no lefs curiofity there than at Vienna. The Princefs Chriftina, and two other royal Polifh Princeffes who were with the Electorefs, their fifter, on account of the war commenced between Saxony and Pruffia, honoured me with their attention, and engaged me in their hunting party. Durinij our ftay, which was not long, and prefents nothing particular
cular

fo·

to cor

the

ılar, we ſpent our time in pleaſures and ·ntertainments. We left that place to re-pair to Lunéville, where Staniſlaus Leck-zinſki, the titular King of Poland, held his Court.

I could not help being filled with reſpect, admiration, and aſtoniſhment, at ſeeing this venerable Prince, who, after ſuch an agi-tated life, after having undergone the moſt fatal reverſes of fortune, ſtill preſerved, at the age of eighty years, all the faculties of his ſoul, and employed them with ſo much energy to promote the happineſs of his new ſubjects. I was ſtruck with his noble aſ-pect, his mild and affable look, his ſerene and ſtately deportment. I immediately re-collected the impreſſion he made at firſt ſight upon Charles XII. It is known, that this extraordinary monarch, after having converſed with him a quarter of an hour, ſaid to the generals who compoſed his reti-nue, This is the man who ſhall be King of Poland.

Poland. It is alfo known, how Charles kept his word;—how Staniflaus, after the difgraces of his protector, faw himfelf ftripped of that crown to which he had only afpired through his confcioufnefs of the good he might do to his own country ; how, when he was called back again to the throne, an adverfe faction, fupported by foreigners, rendered the efforts and hopes of the foundeft part of the nation ufelefs and vain. The dangers are likewife well known to which he was expofed ; and the difguifes he was obliged to fubmit to, to effect an efcape from his enemies. It is known too, that, at laft, peace having fecured him in the tranquil poffeffion of the dukedoms of Lorraine and Bar, he carefully employed himfelf to make thofe people lofe the remembrance of their ancient mafters. Need I tell here all that he did for that purpofe? I will only fay, that his buildings at Nancy and Lunéville appeared to me far fuperior to all that I had feen in many other courts.

c   At

At our arrival, this monarch received us
with that bounty and affability which gained him every heart; and being of his own
country, we were, by his order, lodged in
his palace.

With this Prince lived the famous Bébé,
till then confidered as the moft extraordinary dwarf that ever was feen; who was,
indeed, of a perfectly proportioned fhape,
with very pleafing features, but who (I am
forry to fay it, for the honour of our fpecies)
had, both in his mind and way of thinking,
all the defects commonly attributed to us.
-He was at that time about thirty; when
meafured, it appeared that I. was much
fhorter.

At our firft interview he fhewed much
fondnefs and friendfhip towards me; but
when he perceived that I preferred the company and converfation of perfons of fenfe to
his own, and above all, when he faw that
the

the King took pleasure in my company, he
conceived against me the most violent jea-
lousy and hatred; so that, had it not been
for a kind of miracle, I could not have es-
caped his fury.

One day we were both in the apartment
of his Majesty. This Prince, having much
caressed me, and asked several questions, to
which I gave satisfactory answers, testified
his pleasure and approbation in the most
affectionate manner; then addressing Bébé,
said to him:—You see, Bébé what a differ-.
ence there is between Joujou and you! He
is amiable, chearful, entertaining, and full of
knowledge; whereas you are but a little
machine. At these words, I saw fury sparkle
in his eyes; he answered nothing, but his
countenance and blush proved enough that
he was violently agitated. A moment
after, the King being gone to his closet,
Bébé availed himself of that instant to exe-
cute his revengeful projects; and slily approaching,

proaching, feized me by the waift, and endeavoured to pufh me into the fire. Luckily
I laid hold with both hands of an iron hook,
by which in chimneys, the fhovels and
tongs are kept upright, and thus I prevent-
ed his wicked defign.   The noife I made
in defending myfelf, brought back the King,
who came to my affiftance, and faved me
from that imminent danger. He afterwards
called for his fervants, put Bébé into their
hands, bade them inflict on him a cor-
poral punifhment proportioned to his fault,
and ordered him never to appear in his prefence any more.

In vain did I intercede in behalf of the
unhappy Bébé, I could not fave him the firft
part of his fentence; and as for the other, his
Majefty did not confent to revoke it but
upon condition he fhould beg my pardon.
Bébé, with much reluctance, fubmitted to
this humiliation, which very likely made on
him a deeper impreffion.   In effect, he fell
fick

fick a fhort time after, and died. Every
body attributed his death to his jealoufy,
and to the vexation which the difference
that was faid to be between us had given
him. I fincerely pitied him, and would not
have related this circumftance, but to re-
mark, that the fmallnefs of our ftature does
not prevent us from experiencing the power
of the paffions. Happily for me, when I
have been the fport of them, they never infpired me with any thing contrary to humanity and the laws.

It was during my ftay at Lunéville, that
I had the honour to cultivate an acquaintance with the celebrated Count de Treffan,
who was come to refide there a little while.
He took much notice of me; and the article
Nain in the *Encyclopédie*, with an advantageous mention of me, is written by him.

After having confidered and admired all
that King Staniflaus has done to embellifh

Nancy

Nancy and Lunéville, we took leave of this
good Prince, who gave my benefactrefs letters for the late Queen of France, his
daughter, and repaired to Paris.

I need not fay, that the firft care of the
Countefs Humiefka was to go to Verfailles,
where, as a Polander, fhe eafily got admittance to the Queen, to whom fhe delivered
the letters which the King her father had
honoured her with. This Princefs, who
had preferved much affection for every
thing belonging to her own country, received
her Ladyfhip moft gracioufly. Her Majefty being informed that I was along with
my benefactrefs, wifhed to fee me; fhe was
aftonifhed at my appearance, the fmallnefs
of which fhe had no idea of; and after having afked me many queftions concerning
the King her father, Bébé, Poland, and our
travels, fhe feemed pleafed with my anfwers,
and did me fo much honour as to add, that I
was a little prodigy; that upon what fhe had
feen

seen or ever been told, she till then deemed the individuals of my species as ill-favoured by nature, as much in mind and intellectual faculties as in body, but that I undeceived her in a very advantageous and pleasing manner.

After these obliging words, the Queen, addressing the Countess Humieska, was so kind as to engage her to repeat her visit often, desiring she would bring me with her, and gave orders to admit us whenever we desired it.

On our return to Paris, the curiosity I excited drew many visitors to my protectress; and in less than a week, every person of high rank at Court, every person of fashion in town, waited upon her. I could not help indeed being infinitely flattered by this warm enthusiasm, and the numberless civilities I was honoured with. The Duke of Orleans, especially, having given my pro-

tectress

tectrefs the moft elegant entertainments, was in particular very fond of me, and loaded me with careffes and prefents. I can even fay, that, during our ftay at Paris, this amiable Prince did not pafs a fingle day without giving me new teftimonies of his politenefs,

I fhould be deficient in gratitude towards the Count Oginfki, Grand General of Lithuania, who at that time lived at Paris, if I forgot to mention the particular regard he fhewed to me. His Lordfhip, who came conftantly to pay his vifits to my protectrefs, made much of me, and carried his complaifance fo far as to teach me the firft principles of mufic; an art, in which, as a man of rank, he had made a very aftonifhing progrefs. On feeing that I was intent upon it, and imagining I had a tafte for it, he engaged my benefactrefs to give me for a mafter the celebrated Gavinies, who taught me to play on the violin, and afterwards on the

the guittar; a talent which often folaces me in
moments of trouble and inquietude, infeparable from a fituation like mine. But to return
to the Count Oginfki : This nobleman took
pleafure in having me near him; and I remember one day when he gave a grand
banquet to feveral of the moft diftinguifhed
ladies, he put me in an urn in the corner
of the chamber; and feizing a favourable
opportunity, I overfet the flowers which
enveloped my prifon, when my fudden appearance caufed no fmall fhare of wonder
and furprize among the guefts.

The ecftafy I excited, with all that was
related about my figure, gave rife to an in-
cident, which, had not the Queen inter-
pofed, might have proved of difagreeable
confequence to the Polifh ladies who travel
in France; as you will fee:—

It had happened by chance, that the
Duchefs of Modena, a Princefs of the royal

blood

blood of France, had not been at any of the
entertainments to which I had been invited.
However, her Grace had heard much of
me, and all that she had been told excited
a strong propensity to see me. Her rank
not permitting her to pay the first visit to
the Countess Humieska, she determined to
write to her, and require her company at a
rout which she gave; and as I was the principal person she desired to see, she added to
the card, *especially*, *do not forget to bring
Joujou.*

The Countess Humieska, who possesses
all the sentiments correspondent to her illus-
trious birth; and whose rank, beauty, and
wealth, had drawn on her every where the
most flattering distinctions, was greatly of-
fended at such an invitation; and not thinking proper to gratify a curiosity disclosed in
so awkward and uncomplaisant a manner,
answered, she was very sorry she could not
comply with her Grace's commands; she was
engaged

engaged on that day and the following, fo she could not fay when she might have that honour.

The Duchefs of Modena, who under-ftood perfectly well the meaning of this an-fwer, was very much incenfed, and fpoke and complained of it to every one she met; she even went fo far as to carry her com-plaints to the Queen, imagining that her Majefty, being a Polander, would blame my benefactrefs for it.

.I could almoft believe that the Queen, who had a great regard for the perfons of her own nation, inwardly thought that the Countefs Humiefka was right. However, wishing to fettle a trifle, which, though flight in its principle, might terminate in caufing fome uneafinefs to my benefactrefs, she fent for her, and engaged her to pay a vifit to the Duchefs of Modena. The Countefs anfwered, that through refpect for her

Majefty's orders, fhe would go, but certainly would not take Joujou thither; upon which the Queen, forefeeing that fuch a vifit might only widen the breach, dropped the converfation; and at the end of the vifit, invited the Countefs Humiefka to come and breakfaft with her Majefty two days after, bringing me with her. She fent afterwards another invitation to the Dutchefs of Modena for the fame day, without making known to either of thefe ladies that they were to meet one another.

On the appointed day we waited upon the Queen, and arrived firft. But what a furprife was it to us, when fome minutes after we heard the name of the Duchefs of Modena announced! This Princefs, no lefs aftonifhed than we, came, however, to herfelf very foon; and after fhe had paid her duty to the Queen, fhe and the Countefs faluted each other with the ufual compliments; and, as if nothing had happened, re-
ciprocally

ciprocally declared the pleafure they had to
fee, and the defire they had had to know
one another. The Dutchefs even went fo
far as not to take notice of me for fome
minutes; but foon banifhing this conftraint,
her careffes, praifes, and eagernefs, proved
how great her enthufiafm was.

This adventure, though trivial, made me
the topic of curiofity for the moment, and
I was honoured by a vifit from the late
Princefs of Anhault, dowager to the prefent
Emprefs of Ruffia; a Monarch, not lefs the
admiration of Europe from her diftinguifhed
virtues, than by the glory of her reign, and
the bravery of her troops, fo often crowned
wlth victory in their auguft Sovereign's
caufe!

We continued to be vifited and entertained by every one of the moft confiderable
amongft the nobility and financiers. Mr.
Bouret efpecially, the farmer general, fo
much

much renowned for his ambition, exceffes, and extravagancies, gave an entertainment, in which, to fhow that it was for my fake, he caufed every thing, even the plate, the fpoons, knives and forks, to be proportioned to my fize, and the difhes, confifting of ortolans, becaficos, and other fmall game of this kind, to be ferved up on difhes adapted to them. It was about this time that I got acquainted with the celebrated Demoifelle Clairon, who has fince rendered me the greateft fervices.

We fpent, thus agreeably, more than a year at Paris, in all the pleafures which that capital offers to foreigners; and the lively humour, the chearfulnefs and politenefs of its inhabitants, made our ftay delightful. The time at length came, when we were to leave that place, from whence we fet off for Holland.

Every body knows how the foul of a traveller is impreffed by the novelty of the ſcenes which this country affords. It was then the month of May, a feaſon in which it preſents the moſt agreeable appearance; and I was ſtruck with it in ſo lively a manner, that notwithſtanding the ſameneſs ſo juſtly complained of, I cannot recal to my mind without emotion the ſenſations I then felt. It would be repeating what has been ſaid a thouſand times, if I undertook to deſcribe it; I will then confine myſelf to ſay, that when we arrived at the Hague, this aſtoniſhing village, which may vie with cities of the firſt rank, the Counteſs Humieſka was received in the moſt affable and polite manner by his Highneſs the Prince Stadtholder and his family, who did their utmoſt to make her ſtay agreeable. We, however, made but few acquaintance there; and not being able to ſtay long in Holland, we employed ourſelves in viewing the curioſities with which this country abounds; and at laſt, after having taken leave of the Stadtholder, my benefactreſs took her route

through

through Germany, and we reached War-.
faw.

My return to my native country made
much noife : I had not yet been feen in the
capital, but was preceded by the reputation
I had acquired in my travels, and for which
I was indebted to the generous care of my
benefactrefs. Befides, I had improved much
during my ftay in foreign countries ; and, as
Paris had given me fomewhat of that eafy
politenefs which graces manners, and en-
hances the lighteft prattle, I was fo happy as
to perceive that many perfons, by whom at
firft I was looked upon only as an object of
mere curiofity, fought my fociety, becaufe
they took pleafure in my converfation. Em-
boldened by this notice, I went oftener to
the affemblies than I had done ; and, wifhing
to enlarge the circle of my acquaintance, I
cultivated an intimacy with feveral young
gentlemen of my age, whofe company feem-
to me more gay and interefting than that of
                                        thofe

thofe who habitually frequented the Countefs Humiefka's houfe.

I had infpired my protectrefs with confidence enough to allow me a reafonable liberty, of which I availed myfelf to go fre-
quently to the Play. I had always been an
admirer of it; but now new fenfations which
began to rife in me, increafed its charms.
No longer did I repair thither to admire the
finenefs of the play, or the abilities of the
performers. The fhow itfelf attracted me;
the concourfe of fpectators, but women
above all, who ftirring up in me fome kind
of new emotions, made me attend the Theatre with a degree of rapture. Till then I
had lived almoft without conceiving any
difference between the fexes; but from the
inquietude, the agitation, and the trouble
which the prefence of a female caufed in
me, I could no longer conceal to myfelf,
that on this enchanting fex depends all our
happinefs; yet was I not able to define in
what and how it might be promoted.

The

The theatre was alfo the general ren-
dezvous of my young friends. They had
all the indiscretion of their age, and indulged without scruple the impulse of their
brisk and sprightly imagination. By incef-
santly talking of their pleasures past, or in
project, it was not long before they supplied
me with the knowledge I wanted, and gave
a fixed bias to defires till then confufed and
incoherent. Women, befides, by their con-
tinual railleries at the shortness of my sta-
ture, their pleasantries on my refervednefs and
circumspection, completely cured me of that
timidity, which feemed, as it were ascribed
to my fize. My head being filled with the
idea of them, my heart strongly agitated by
the change lately operated in me, I viewed
the objects under afpects more lively and interefting; I wished to love; I did fo already.
Woman, in my eyes, had taken quite a new
form. They excited my admiration, my
fenfibility, my defires: but it was sufficient
to be a woman, that title gave her a right

to

to my rifing paffion: I was fond of the fex,
without choice or diftinction; I loved them
all.—In a word, at the age of twenty-five I
was like other young lads at fifteen.

Thefe emotions, quite new to me, had
their charms; and, perhaps, I had been hap-
pier, if I could have been contented with
experiencing them, without feeking how to
gratify defires which every day grew more
preffing. Unhappily, fuch a refiftance is
not in the nature of man; preffed by the
warmth of my conftitution, I wifhed to fix
my views upon a particular object. How
much was my mind mortified on reflecting
upon my ftature; which I confidered as an
infurmountable obftacle to the happinefs I
longed for with fo much ardour! What,
faid I to myfelf, the moft referved women take me upon their lap! they embrace me, they beftow upon me the moft
tender careffes, they ufe me like a child!
How can I hazard, in fuch circumftances,
a declaration

a declaration at which they will only laugh, while I shall remain covered with eternal ridicule ? It was not an easy matter to make my pride agree with my desires. The farther I was from having the common size of other men, the more lively I wished that difference might be forgotten, and that I might be treated like them. But experience has taught me that I thought as a child. I was ignorant of the effect such wonderful things may produce : above all, I knew not, forgive me, ye fair! to what height female curiosity might soar:—I soon knew it.

There was then at Warsaw, amongst the French comedians, an actress highly distinguished for her talents in the character of a waiting-maid. A certain mixture of tenderness and vivacity rendered her infinitely interesting; and though not regularly handsome, yet she possessed all that was requisite to please and seduce. I always saw her with new pleasure, and openly preferred her

to

to all others. One night, when she had made on me a most particular impression, on going out of the play-house, I met with one of my friends, to whom, intending some relaxation, I proposed a walk; he desired me to excuse him, and confessed that he was going to sup at the little ***, precisely the same actress. Ah! exclaimed I with emotion, are you acquainted with her? How happy are you!—So may you be, when you please, answered my giddy-young spark: I will introduce you to her, as my friend, and you may be sure to be well received. This offer I accepted with transport, and the very next day I was introduced, and welcomed in a manner equal to what I had been made to hope. This visit passed away merrily, and when I retired, she most earnestly invited me often to repeat it.

With what eagerness did I avail myself of this invitation! How long the moments seemed which were to bring that of seeing her!

her ! With what regret did I see those fly
away which I spent with her ! I was bold
enough to declare my paffion for her; she
seemed to partake of it, and for a while my
illusion made me happy.   Pleased, nay, in-
toxicated with this amour, I avoided my
young friends,—wanted to enjoy within myself my imaginary felicity,—devoted to my
young miftrefs all the moments I could fteal
from the decency and duty impofed upon
me by the bounty of my benefactrefs.   Let
these details be forgiven me; in writing thefe
memoirs, I not only mean to defcribe my
fize and its proportions, I would likewife
follow the unfolding of my fentiments, the
affections of my foul; I would fpeak openly;
rather tell what I felt than what I did, and
demonftrate that, if I can upbraid nature
with having refufed me a body like that
of other men, she has made me ample
amends, by endowing me with a fenfibility
which, it is true, difplayed itfelf rather
late, but, even in my conftitutional warmth,
                                    fpread

ſpread a teint of happineſs, the remembrance
of which I enjoy with gratitude and a feeling heart.

But to return to my charmer, the Abi-
gail:—Our conneÄion did not laſt long; I
was ſincere in my attachment, and imagining myſelf beloved, ſhe made me happy.
Therefore, how great muſt be my aſtoniſhment, when one day on meeting by chance
the very ſame young man who had introduced me to her, I was told that my little
intrigue was known to every body, and
ſpoken of publicly; that they bantered my
diſcretion; and ſhe, whom I thought the moſt
intereſted in ſecreſy, did not ſcruple openly
to laugh at my paſſion and eagerneſs, at the
tumultuous emotions ſhe had excited in me;
that ſhe even gloried in it, and produced as
no ſmall proof of her merit, to have pro-
voked in a man of my ſize a manner of
being apparently ſo little ſuited to him.
This diſcovery ſunk me down, by humbling

                        my

my pride; I thought I loved fincerely, I had hoped to be as fincerely beloved; and it was not without extreme grief I faw the veil fall, and my illufion difpelled.

My benefactrefs, who was not ignorant of this affair, fent to me a very grave, wife, and fenfible man, in whom I had the greateft confidence; he ftrongly remonftrated to me on the irregularity of my behaviour, and fet forth the fatal confequences into which I was likely to be hurried away. His reflections affected me; I promifed never more to frequent the young men whofe difcourfes and bad examples had feduced me; and, by the regularity of my conduct, I foon regained the kindnefs of the Countefs Humiefka, and of her fociety.

I had no occafion to repent it. My life was more quiet and happy. The effervefcence of a juvenile conftitution had procured me fome pleafures; but it was not

long

long before I felt the vacuum they left behind them. I then began to perceive that
fentiment, reciprocal fentiment only, can
give animation and livelinefs to pleafures,
which without it are nought. I began to
comprehend that efteem and confidence
only can give birth to a permanent love.
In the friendfhip and converfation of wife
perfons I fought after a compenfation, and
eafily found it.

At that time Warfaw was the fcene of
rejoicings and amufement. Staniflaus II.
had lately afcended the throne of Poland;
and this Prince, on whofe virtues and ac-
complifhments I need not expatiate, as they
are known to all thofe who had the honour
to approach him either as a King or a private
man, was applying himfelf to retrieve thofe
innumerable calamities which a feries of
troubles and agitations had occafioned. By
his patronage, the arts and fciences were

flourifhing;

flourifhing; he gained the affections of his greateft Lords, who flocked round his perfon, to evince their attachment.

In the midft of thefe rejoicings his Majefty came to fup, on the twelfth night, with the princefs Lubomifka, where I attended the Countefs Humiefka. The cake being opened, I was chofen king, and had the honour to enter into converfation with his Majefty, and intreated his permiffion, to lay afide in his prefence the prerogative of my newly attained royalty. This propofition from me, afforded great diverfion to the King, who turned to the Countefs, my-benefactrefs, and deigned to fignify that my behaviour gave him much pleafure, and faid he was inclined as a mark of his royal favour to beftow an eftate upon me. But my protectrefs's countenance too plainly befpoke her difapprobation of his generous offer, for it to take place.

In this ftate of tranquillity my days glided away, and I thought that no kind of vexation could trouble fo happy a life. I was then very far from forefeeing that this delicate and tender fentiment upon which was grounded my expectation of a future felicity, fhould one day be the caufe of difquietude and bitternefs of heart, and would fo powerfully overwhelm my exiftence. But before I enter into the particulars of thefe events, which I fhall always behold as the moft interefting of my life, I beg leave to acquaint my reader with fome circumftances which belong to the hiftory of my fifter, whofe death I heard of nearly at this epoch.

Anaftafia Boruwlafki was feven years younger than myfelf, and of fo fhort a ftature, that fhe could exactly ftand under my arm; but this can be no matter of aftonifhment, when what I faid before is remembered, that fhe was only two feet two inches high at the time of her death. Afto-

infhing

nifhing as fhe was, for the fhortnefs of her
perfon, and the extreme regular proportions of her fhape, with which the niceft
fculptor could not have found fault, fhe
was ftill more fo by the qualities of her
heart, and the gentlenefs of her difpofition.
She was of a brown complexion, with fine
black eyes, well circled eye-brows, very
thick hair, and fo much gracefulnefs in all
fhe did, that added new charms to her
figure. Her temper was lively and chearful; her heart, feeling and beneficent. She
could not fee a fuffering fellow-creature,
without feeking to give relief. The Caftelane Kaminfka, a very rich lady, was both
a friend and a protectrefs to her. She had
taken her to her houfe, expreffed for her an
unbounded tendernefs, refufed her nothing;
and the little Anaftafia availed herfelf of
that afcendency, to gratify her own heart,
which incited her to generofity.

My fifter, like me, had been fo happy
as to feel thofe tender affections which dif-
fufe

fuſe ſo many charms over our lives, and
the ſweetneſs of which does ſo well coun-
terpoiſe the troubles, the inquietudes and
contradictions which they make us ſuffer.
At twenty, Anaſtaſia was in love, and with
ſo much the more paſſion, that her attachment was grounded upon the only pleaſure
of contributing to the happineſs of him who
was the object of it. She had neither fears,
nor ſorrows, nor remorſes to endure; and
thus ſhe might have lived happy, had not
jealouſy overpowered her, and too often
troubled her repoſe. It was not difficult for
her benefactreſs to perceive her inclination:
ſhe mentioned it to her; and this ingenuous,
tender and feeling heart did not conceive
the ſentiments which a young officer of a
very handſome ſhape and fine figure, who
frequented the houſe, had inſpired her with.
This young gentleman, though of a good
family, was not rich; Anaſtaſia knew it, and
endeavouring to find the means of ſerving
him without hurting his delicacy, ſhe contrived

trived to engage him to play at piquet with her; and generally obliging him to play deep, she contrived always to lose, and thus joined the pleasure of doing him good, to that of avoiding his expressions of gratitude. I know not how far my sister's sensibility would have carried her, if during an excursion to Leopold she had not been seized with the small-pox. Unfortunately for me and for her friends, the disorder was without remedy. Recourse was had in vain to all the helps of the medical art; and within two days she died, with the same tranquillity of soul, the same calmness of mind, nay, the same philosophy with which she had lived. I cannot recollect this sad event without shedding tears, for the loss of a sister and of a friend. Her benefactress was inconsolable, and during many days her health was in danger. She gave the strictest orders that nobody should ever speak to her of her dear Anastasia; even desired me not to come to see her, lest my presence

should

fhould open again deep wounds too difficult to be healed; thus I was deprived of
the fatisfaction of mingling my tears with
,hers, and of fhewing her my warm, though
infufficient, gratitude for all that fhe had
done to her young and little friend.

Other cares and anxities foon fucceeded
thofe which this lofs had caufed me. I
come now to the moft interefting epoch
of my life, thofe moments, which, being
fraught with new ideas, new defires, pleafures far different from thofe I had known,
brought likewife new troubles and new
difficulties to which I never thought I
fhould be expofed. The Countefs Humiefka's bounty feemed for ever to fecure me
from want. As her ladyfhip's favour had
drawn on me the confideration and regard
not only of every perfon in her houfe, but
even of all the quality that compofed her
fociety, I did not forefee, nor did I find in
my heart, the fear of ever becoming un-
worthy of her regard. I was careffed,

D 4   fondled

fondled and cherifhed; nothing was wanting to my happinefs; and I enjoyed it with fo much the more fecurity, that not knowing reverfes, I foolifhly thought never to endure any. On the other fide, reafon and good counfels having brought me back to more quiet fentiments; I thought thofe tumultuous paffions, which for a while had fo vehemently agitated me, were for ever calmed. I imagined that, by confining my affections to marks of gratitude towards fo many perfons who liberally beftowed their kindnefs upon me, I fhould lead a peaceful life; and that, reclaimed from love and its chimeras, my renouncing it for ever would make me amends for the pains it had occafioned me. But I knew not my own heart; and thefe fine refolutions vanifhed, when I faw a young perfon whom my benefactrefs had lately taken into her houfe as a lady in waiting, or companion.

Ifalina was defcend from French parents, long fettled in Warfaw, where they enjoyed

enjoyed a happy mediocrity. It is a cuf-
tom in Poland for the Lords, as well as
Ladies of quality, to take young perfons
of good birth, who are brought up at their
own charge, and afterwards provided for,
either by admitting. them into their houfehold, giving them in marriage, or procur-
ing them civil or military employments.
This ancient ufage had its origin in the
wide difproportion of fortunes amongft the
nobility. According to the conftitution of
the country, all noblemen may afpire to
the crown, which is elective; fo that the
richeft of them attach to themfelves a vaft
number of creatures, who upon occafion
may fupport their pretenfions.

Be that as it may, my benefactrefs had
only confulted her own heart, when fhe
took Ifalina; and this young lady poffeffed
all the requifites to intereft and pleafe her.
Let me be excufed from defcribing what
fhe appeared in my eyes; and befides, fuch

as

as regard only the figure in the choice of their conforts, know very little of the human heart. To live together, to have for each other that mutual efteem which alone can make us happy, more lafting qualities are requifite. Being at this day a father, having found in my wife a fincere friend, who partakes of my pains and pleafures, a fond mother who only delights in educating her' children, I know how to fet a proper value on thofe advantages fo much fought after, though they only are gifts which nature blindly diftributes. Yet I muft own, there is a perfonal beauty which difclofes that of the foul; and when we meet with fuch tender, fweet and lively countenances, which, being ftrangers to diffimulation and deceit, exhibit in their features the motions they feel, the impreffions they receive, we muft acknowledge, at the very firft moment, that perfrns fo happily endowed are worthy of all our attachment. It is among women efpecially that this ineftimable qua-

lity

lity is to be found, which fets off their charms fo advantageoufly: they poffefs it, notwithftanding all the obftacles that are oppofed to it; though the aim of their education inceffantly be to inftruct them how to diffemble their fentiments, and conceal their natural affections. May I have refolution and wifdom enough to overcome this prejudice in training up my children! But I fee the evil, and know not the remedy, or rather have not courage enough to ufe it.

It was, however, young Ifalina's beauty. which ftruck me at firft fight, and fubdued my heart. But if from that moment the impreffion was deep and indelible, what a new force did my fentiments receive, when living in the fame houfe, and having every day opportunities to fee her, I could freely admire her lively and chearful converfation, when I difcovered in her a perpetual vivacity, and that native meeknefs which was

the

the plain index of a feeling heart! From
this time my happinefs was affixed to her
fate; without fear I difcovered in me all the
fymptoms of a violent paffion; and though
I forefaw the numberlefs obftacles I had to
òvercome, yet I did not give up my enter-
prize, and hoped that by dint of perfever-
ance and attention, they fhould be at laft
furmounted.

How different was this paffion from the
tumultuous fenfations which had before dif-
turbed me! I was in love, but a love accompanied with that refpect and diffidence
which are infeparable from a true paffion.
My only defire was to fpend my life with
the object that caufed it; and whereas formerly I had been determined only by the
allurements of pleafure and perfonal fatif-
faction, which, leaving the heart empty, and
bringing diftafte, flatters our pride but faintly,
I felt that the end at which I truly aimed,
was the happinefs of the perfon to whom I

was

was attached; and that, if I could fucceed
to make her happy, there would not be any
thing wanting to my own felicity.

My benefactrefs, charmed at the qualities fhe difcovered in her young favourite,
took a moft particular liking and intereft
in her behalf. Living under the fame roof,
and feeing her every day with that fweet
familiarity which my fize, her youth and
innocence feemed to authorize, I did not
lofe a fingle opportunity of approaching
her; I had no other delight than to fee and
admire, to love her fecretly. Much time
paffed before I could refolve to acquaint
her with my fentiments. Every day I
formed this refolution; but every day the
reflections of my mind difcovered obftacles that were more and more invincible,
and my fpeech expired ere it reached my
lips. Whilft I fuffered every lady to take
me on her lap, and fubmitted to their fondnefs and careffes, I was anxioufly cautious
left

left Ifalina fhould do the fame; I fhunned her notice, either with a ferious look, or by ftealing away from her. She often complained of being the only one I loved not; but how little did fhe know the inmoft dealings of my heart! When I would have given my life to enjoy a fingle one of her careffes as a friend, I fcorned to receive all thofe fhe would lavifh on me as on a child: nay, by humbling my pride to the utmoft, they ended with caufing in me fo real and violent a pain, that I cannot defcribe it. It was then I bitterly felt all the difadvantages of my fize. Then all the praifes I was loaded with on every other fide, could not make me amends for the inconveniences I found myfelf liable to. It was then I confidered it as the fole obftacle to the only good that could attach me to life: to be upon a level with other men, I would have facrificed both the fondnefs of my benefactrefs; and the bounty, even I will fay, the confideration with which the King and

the

the Nobles of his court vouchfafed to honour me.

It was not only the fear of becoming unacceptable to Ifalina that dejected my mind. I apprehended that, fhould I fucceed in winning her affection, could I engage her to lay afide prejudices, and be refolved concerning the union of her fate to mine, there would ftill remain many difficulties to overcome, either to gain her parents' confent, without which there was no hope left for me, or to obtain the fanction of my benefactrefs who undoubtedly would think this marriage ridiculous, and by all means oppofe it. This laft was not the leaft powerful obftacle. Befides my being bound to the Countefs Humiefka by fentiments of the moft tender refpect and heartfelt gratitude, I had no fortune; I was totally indebted to her beneficence for my eafy circumftances. I had, therefore, to fear left I fhould lofe it by marrying againft her will;

will; I had reason to be afraid of involving in my misfortunes a young person, who, though without fortune herself, had by her youth, education, figure, and, above all, by the protection of our common benefactress, a right to an advantageous match.

These reflections did not all occur to my mind at first. During more than one year I had been fully taken up with the delight of loving and daily seeing the object of my affections; but at length, when I was come to that point so natural, wherein to speak of our love is irresistibly necessary, they crouded in my imagination, and filled me with anguish and melancholy. They, indeed, ought to have made me renounce my passion; but do we reason when in love? My health became visiby impaired; I was uneasy and anxious beyond conception; in short, so violent was my situation, that not being able to remain in this cruel uncertainty, I determined on declaring my

passion,

paſſion, and waited only for a favourable opportunity, which ſoon preſented itſelf.

One evening when I had been more ſad
and dejeƈted than uſual, chance, or rather
the attraƈtion that kept me faſt to Iſalina,
made me ſtay the laſt in the drawing-room.
I then formed the reſolution of opening my
heart to her, which gave me ſuch a look of
trouble and perplexity, that ſhe could not
help being ſtruck with.   " Pray what is the
matter, Joujou?" ſaid ſhe to me, with the
moſt ſtriking look of concern and pity.
" What is the ſorrow that preys upon you,
and which you ſo artfully conceal? Is there
nobody in whom you can place confidence
enough to pour out your heart? You aƈt
unkindly with your friends."—And comes
this reproach from you, anſwered I with
warmth, from you, the only cauſe of all
my grief?—I wiſhed to go on, but letting
my head fall upon her lap, I could only liſp
the words love—paſſion—misfortune.---

At

At firſt, Iſalina's heart ſtartled at the pitiful ſtate ſhe ſaw me in; but ſoon recovering from her ſurprize, ſhe only found the ſcene ridiculous.—Indeed, Joujou, ſaid ſhe, you are a child, and I cannot but laugh at your extravagance. Did I ever forbid you to love me? On the contrary, did I not always upbraid you for your indifference to me?

I did not expect ſuch an anſwer, I own; I had much difficulty in making her underſtand that I did not love her as a child, and would not be loved like a child. At this ſhe burſt into laughter, told me I knew not what I ſaid, and left the apartment.

More content with having made my declaration, than minding the manner it had been received, I wholly gave myſelf over to the pleaſure of knowing that the object of my fondneſs was appriſed of the paſſion ſhe had cauſed me to breathe. I reaſoned with myſelf, that now ſhe might eaſily interpret

my

my meloncholy, my grief, and my reſerved-
neſs towards her; that ſhe could not but
attribute them to a ſtrong and deep ſentiment. I ventured to hope, that ſuch a
ſentiment would ſpeak in my behalf, and
plead my cauſe to a delicate and feeling
heart. But the ſucceeding days plainly
ſhewed that I was miſtaken. She inceſſantly bantered me; and indulging herſelf
in the gaiety of her imagination, the more
I endeavoured to diſplay my ſentiments,
and to ſpeak to her as a man, the more ſhe
delighted in ridiculing them, and treated
me like a child. She aſked me—whither I
imagined her like my young aĉreſs? How
many days longer would my ſentiments
laſt?—I could not return any anſwer; I left
her, and inveighed againſt her injuſtice, and
my misfortune.

Unable any longer to reſiſt the heavy
melancholy that had ſeized me through ſuch
uſage, my ſtrength failed me, & kept my

room

room more than two months. She some-
times inquired after my fituation. I feized
the firft opportunity of fpeaking to her in
private. She affured me fhe had been very
much concerned at it: and that if I had
liftened more to reafon, if I had loved her as
fhe thought fhe had merited, I might have
fpared her this trouble. She promifed me
fince I was fo much affected, fhe would
banter me no more upon my love. She
hoped that on my part, I would entertain
more calm fentiments towards her.

What comfort did this fpeech infufe into
my foul, being fo tenderly expreffed, it affured my happinefs; I then thought I had
made fome impreffion on the tender heart
of Ifalina. And indeed how could I fail,
my love guided by fincerity, and my mif-
fortunes proved my difintereftednefs. But
thefe raptures were foon interrupted by the
Countefs; fhe was fully informed of, and faw
with conern my affection for Ifalina, fhe

was

was determined to ufe her utmoft endeavours to fruftrate our intentions. She fent
Ifalina immediately to her parents, and at
the fame time kept me fhut up in my
room for a fortnight together. Thus con-
fined, fhe difcharged my footman, and put
another in his place whom fhe thought fhe
could rely on; but contrary to her expectations he was entirely at my difpofal; for by
his means I eftablifhed a correfpondence
with my beautiful Ifalina.

Caglioftro, at the inftigation of the
Countefs, came to me a few days after, and
earneftly folicited me to appeafe my benefactrefs by renouncing Ifalina.--Without the
leaft hefitation, I boldly declared, I would
fooner part with my life. I fhall take this
opportunity of relating how this Caglioftro
had infinuated himfelf into the good graces
of the Countefs Humiefka.

This adventurer having made a great
noife in France, on his arrival at Warfaw,

saw, artfully introduced himself to the Prince Poninſki under the character of a great chymiſt, in poſſeſſion of the philoſopher's ſtone, or art of making gold. But his fame was of a ſhort duration; for the Count Poninſki, a literati, watched him attentively through his operations, and clearly proved him an ignoramus or rather an impoſtor. During his diſgrace he was favourably received by the Counteſs my Benefactreſs, not with any confidence of his ſkill in the philoſopher's ſtone, but rather as a phyſician to who ſhe confided the care of her health. But here ſhe was moſt egregiouſly deceived; for in a ſhort time, ſhe was reduced to an alarming and dangerous ſtate, which her brother the Count Rewiſki perceiving, endeavoured to remove her ill placed confidence in a ſtranger, and made uſe of his power to baniſh him the kingdom. The number of follies this man has propagated is ſufficiently known throughout all Europe.

The

The Countefs of Humiefka perceiving me determined, became furious, and fetting me at liberty, declared I had only to chufe either toe rnounce my paffion for Ifalina, or quit her houfe immediately: I preferred the latter, as will be feen in the two follow-letters to my dear Ifalina; and thefe only I fhall trouble my readers with in all our correfpondence.

Joujou to Ifalina.

November 20, 1780.

MY captivity, my charming friend, is now at an end; I have facrificed all for your fake, and if I lofe you I will renounce, yea, I will renounce, life itfelf! This morning one of the principal officers of the houfe came with a meffage from the Countefs to inform me, if I had not changed my refolution, I muft leave the houfe for ever: that is not poffible, I exclaimed; but reflecting

on

on what conditions alone I could remain, I calmly anfwered, I was ready to depart; but I intreated he would tell my bene-factrefs how fincerely I was affected in incurring her refentment, and befought her to pardon my oppofing her will; which nothing could have urged me to, but the dread of forfeiting all my hopes of happinefs; and that the kindnefs with which fhe had formerly treated me, fhould never be erafed from my memory.

I am now at large; but on beholding the houfe where I had fo long been the darling, I burft into tears; how painful a fituation to a heart like mine; who while loft in love, bears the reproach of ingratitude.

I know nor where to direct my courfe; pennylefs, a forlorn wanderer, my fituation is dreadful; love, it is thou alone can fupport me: yes, love infpired me to addrefs myfelf to Prince Cafimir the King's
brother,

brother; his affability, his gentle manners, you are well acquainted with. You are not ignorant how much he interefted himfelf in all that concerned me. I was not deceived in my expectations: he knew all except my departure, at which he was much furprized. Make yourfelf eafy, Joujou, fays he, you fhall not want: I will never forfake you; come and fee me foon. I will importune the King in your behalf; you know he loves you, and I am fure he will protect you. Thefe kind expreffions have animated my drooping fpirits. Dear Ifalina, be kind, and we fhall yet be happy. But permit me to fee you—to fpeak to you—and repeat a thoufand and a thoufand times, with my laft breath, you are all the hope the delight of the faithful and tender

Joujou.

Joujou to Ifalina.

November 27, 1780.

The Prince fent for me this morning, my charming friend. . How can I exprefs

E   to

to you my grateful fentiments for his numerous favours? he afked me if I would
return to the Countefs Humiefka, and he
would ufe all his influence to foften her; or
if I was refolved to marry my dear Ifalina;
fo he expreffed himfelf. I anfwered him,
that I was exceedingly forry to have forfeit-
ed the protection of the Countefs; but that
my heart could never fubfcribe to her hard
conditions. Obtain then the mother's confent, replied this amiable prince, and all will
yet be well. You fee, my lovely friend, they
think your fentiments fympathize with mine.
I durft not acknowledge I had not your
confent; that would have fpoiled all. Can
you refufe it me, my kind Ifalina? Can you
harbour a thought that would deftroy the
man who adores you? I am to be prefented
to his Majefty; he has promifed his illuftrious brother to provide for me. Thus all
our anxieties for fubfiftence ceafe: I expect
an annuity. Dart then, my charmer, a ray
of hope, and I will kneel at your mother's
feet: fhe will yield to my fupplications, feeing

ing me so well protected. All my hopes
are concentred in my Isalina's tendernefs;
but confider, that the leaft indifference, the
leaft delay, may deftroy for ever the hopes of
happinefs in your tender and affectionate

Joujou.

I waited upon Isalina's mother, whofe
confent I obtained; I faw my fair friend
again, a friend, whofe inexhauftible ftock of
gaiety makes fo happy a contraft with my
temper, that I foon buried in oblivion all
the vexations I had endured. The Prince
Chamberlain kept his word; he was fo kind
as to prefent me to his Majefty, who approved of my marriage, and granted me an
annuity of an hundred ducats. The Pope's
Nuncio wanted to prevent it, by a ridiculous pretext; but the King prevailed over
this obftacle; and fome time after, the performance of the ceremony broke all the
barriers that had been oppofed to my felicity.

E 2   Yes,

Yes, it is true, I have sacrificed for this happiness—eafe and tranquility. It has been for me the fource of a thoufand inquietudes, refpecting either the fubfiftence of myfelf and family, or that of my children for the future. Yet, for thefe eight years that I have enjoyed it, I have found that nothing in the world is preferable to the fatisfaction of pouring our inquietudes, our hopes, our fears into the bofom of a true friend united to our fate, whofe tender and feeling foul relieves our pains by fharing them, and enlivens our pleafures with a far greater delight.

I Should

I Should have been too happy in my new ftate, if it had been poffible that folely minding the prefent I had not caft an eye on the future; but man is not formed for a pure and perfect felicity; difquietudes poifon his enjoyments; and it but too often happens that from thefe very enjoyments arife his difquietudes. Notwithftanding my inexperience, I foon perceived that the King's favours would hardly be fufficient for our maintenance; and through much delicacy feverely anticipating the neceffities my new confort muft fubmit to, the livelinefs of my fentiments towards her ftill increafed the bitternefs and horror of my reflections. Although accuftomed to the luxury and magnificence which had furrounded us in the houfe of my benefactrefs, yet without grief, and even with a kind of pleafure, we fhould

E 3   have

have embraced a middle ftation of life, the
only one, perhaps, which gives to the tender and delicate fentiments their full fcope
and energy. But the queftion was not of
expences more or lefs confiderable, we were
likely to want even the neceffaries of life;
and I confefs that the idea of feeing a beloved wife involved in mifery, did not long
permit me to enjoy the happinefs of poffeff-
ing her.

It was needful to take fome ftep; but
the choice was fo much the more difficult,
as having received no other education but
fuch as was analogous to my fize, and the
ftation which the Countefs Humiefka feemed to have afcribed to me, I poffeffed at moft
a few agreeable talents, which would not
offer me any refource. In this perplexity,
my protectors were the firft who fuggefted
to me the idea of a fecond journey. The
Prince Chamberlain, efpecially, feconded
this project. He intimated to me, that having

ing been kindly received in the principal
Courts of Europe, when I accompanied my
benefactrefs, they would fee me again with
the fame pleafure ; and on knowing that I was
a father, and without fortune, this pofition
would increafe the intereft I had infpired,
and in a decent manner procure me the
means of leading, at my return, a peaceful
and tranquil life.

I gave myfelf up to this idea.   I fpoke
of it to the King, who not only vouchfafed
to approve of my plan, but, even wifhing
to grant me a particular teftimony of his
bounty, ordered the Mafter of the Horfe to
fupply me with a convenient coach.   Having alfo taken all neceffary meafures, and
being provided with letters of recommendation, I left Warfaw the 21ft of November,
1780, and reached Cracow the 26th in the
evening.

This town, formerly the capital of Poland, and where the coronation of the Kings

was performed, is now no more than a fron-
tier town, upon the viftula, which feparates
what remains of Poland to the Common-
wealth, from that part which the Auftrians
have invaded. An illnefs having befallen
my wife, we were obliged to ftay there.
On her recovery, I fet out for Vienna, notwithftanding the cold was exceffive.

We reached there on the 11th of Fe-
bruary, 1781; but, unluckily for me, death
had juft before deprived the world of the
illuftrious Maria Therefa. A mournful
forrow pervaded the whole town; and, as
if every one had loft his wife, his parent, the
deepeft grief was impreffed on all their features. All public entertainments, even concerts, were fufpended. They only talked
of the lofs that had befallen them; of the
magnanimity with which this heorine had
fupported adverfe events. They recollected
thofe difaftrous times, when, forced to leave
her refidence, and holding her fon in her
arms, fhe had excited, amongft the Hunga-
rians,

rians, that patriotic fermentation which had impelled them to do fo much for her fake. Whilft they expatiated· with complacency upon the means fhe had employed to re-eftablifh her affairs, upon the glorious treaty which put an end to a war apparently threatening her in its origin with a total deftruction; on the other hand, with new regrets, enumerated the pains fhe had fince taken, the cares fhe had been at to reftore fuch of her provinces as had been defolated by war, to render the moft advantageous to her fubjects the peace fhe had procured them..

In the midft of this general mourning, I renewed my acquaintance with moft ot the noblemen I had the honour to fee in my former travels. Even I may venture to fay, that his Excellency the Prince de Kaunitz received my vifit with every mark of benevolence and pleafure. As at that time his Imperial Majefty, Jofeph II. held no court, all the nobility affembled every

evening in the Prince's hotel (where his relation, the C. Clariffa, received the guefts);
he did me fo much favour as to prefent me
to this affembly, and engage me often to
come and fpend the evening. There I had
the honour to become acquainted with his
Excellency Sir Robert Murray Keith, the
Britifh Ambaffador, who has been the principal caufe afterwards of my paffage into
England. There alfo I had occafion to be
convinced, that the great occupations of the
Prince de Kaunitz, his fuperior talents,
known to every one, in comprehending at
one view the moft extenfive and complicate
affairs, in forefeeing all their confequences,
and preventing the events refulting from
them, did not hinder him from looking on
the minuteft objects, the leaft worthy of fix-
ing his attention. For, having fent for the
meafure of my fize, which he had carefully
taken when I was at Vienna, 1761, with the
Countefs Kumiefka, he fhewed to us, that
from that time to 1781, I had grown up-
wards

wards of ten inches. Which appeared as
much furprifing to thofe who, not having
feen me before, did not conceive how, this
moment (1781) being hardly in fize like a
child, I could have been ten inches fhorter;
as to thofe who, having feen me twenty
years before, thought they obferved in me
as much difference, as there is between a
youth of twelve and a grown man of
thirty.

Notwithftanding thefe fine appearances,
and the profeffions of friendfhip I received
every where, my journey did not anfwer
the intended purpofe. My hopes, it is true,
were grounded upon a concert; but though
I muft have waited until the mourning was
over, yet I had ftill new difficulties to overcome, new obftacles to furmount. A crowd
of *Virtuofi* were infcribed on the catalogue,
at the royal theatre; and if I had been
obliged to wait for my turn, I might have
been kept a great way back. Happily for

me,

me, my protectors in general, and especially
Mr. Gunter, Secretary to his imperial Majesty, so much pressed Mr. Dorval, the ma-
nager of the house, that I was preferred before the others; and they were even so kind
as to manage for me, and conduct the concert and the expences.

I was so fortunate as to be honoured
with a numerous assembly, and almost all
the nobility was present. I attempted in a
short speech to express my gratitude to
them; I wanted likewise to make an apo-
logy before that same nobility, who, twenty
years ago, having seen me surrounded with
the eclat of greatness, saw me now reduced to the sad necessity of appearing in
public.

I was at that time very far from thinking, that, through necessity of providing for
the most essential wants of life, I should be
obliged to expose myself to view for money.

ney. The education I had received, the
manner in which I had lived till now, contributed to make me look upon this refource
as beneath me; and though all the perfons
concerned for my welfare endeavoured to
bring me to that refolution, yet I had ftill
much reluctance to take it.   Above all, the
Baron de Breteuil, then ambaffador from
the court of France to that of Vienna, was
inceffantly preffing me thereon.   Do not
' believe,' faid he to me one day, ' my little
' friend, that concerts will always be fuffi-
' cient to anfwer your expences, and to pro-
' cure you a fupport; you muft needs give
' up pride, or choofe mifery; and if you do
' not intend to lead the moft unhappy life;
' if you wifh to enjoy, in future, a ftate of
' tranquillity, it is indifpenfable you fhould
' refolve to make exhibition of yourfelf.'
The next day the Prince de Kaunitz fpoke
to me in the fame manner amidft a crowd-
ed levee. His Excellency Sir Robert Murray Keith was prefent; he prevailed upon
                                        me

me to go over to England, in preference to France, which was the country I intended firſt to viſit. The Prince ſupported this advice, and earneſtly deſired the Ambaſſador to intereſt himſelf for me. His Excellency promiſed me letters of recommendation to the greateſt perſonages at the Britiſh Court; the Prince made him on acknowledgment for it, and aſſured him he would ſeek every opportunity to ſhew him how ſenſible he was of all that was done to his little friend.

If all theſe reaſons did not entirely prevail, at leaſt they acted upon me; and I reſolved to leave Vienna, being ſupplied with the beſt letters of recommendation to many Princes of Germany. But before I ſpeak of the kind welcome I met with in the ſeveral Courts I viſited, I think it a duty to mention the beneficence of the Counteſs Féguetté, who inſiſted on my not ſetting out till I had previouſly made a journey to Preſbourg;

Prefbourg; and not only defrayed all the
expences of this tour, but even added a prefent.   I ftaid there only the neceffary time
to give a concert; and from thence I went
to Lintz, where the Count de Thierheim,
Governor of Low Auftria, and fon-in-law
to the Prince de Kaunitz, loaded me with
kindneffes.   He was fo good as to lend me
for the concert his band of muficians : this
band was compofed of fifteen young men,
all good performers, the eldeft of whom was
not feventeen.   The audience being very
thinly attended, occafioned this to be faid:
Little concert, little mufic, little players, and
little receipt.—I ought not to omit an in-
genious faying of the Countefs de Thierheim, then between fix and feven.   This
fine young lady did not ceafe to look at me
all the concert; when it was over, fhe ran
to her papa, and clinging round his neck,
earneftly begged he would buy her this
little man.—Well ! what would you do with
him, my dear child ? faid the Count to her;
                                    —befides,

—befides, we have no apartment for him.
let that be no obftacle, papa, replied fhe, I
will keep him in mine, will take the utmoft care of him, have the pleafure of dreff-
ing and adorning him, of loading him with
careffes and dainties.—In a word, they had
much ado to perfuade her that it was not
poffible to purchafe the little man like a
doll.

The next place where I ftopped at was
Ratifbon; but not finding the Prince de la
Tour et Taxis, who was then at his eftate
at Tefchen, I went immediately to Munich,
where her Royal Highnefs the Electrefs
Dowager, whom I had the honour to vifit
twenty years before, was very glad to fee
me again, and fhewed me the fame kindnefs as at the time of my former journey.
She perfectly remembered the particular
pleafure her illuftrious hufband had in con-
verfing with me, and the fpecial favour he
had done me, by prefenting me with a chafed
gold

gold box, made by himfelf. She prefented me to His Moft Serene Highnefs, the now reigning Elector. I was often invited to the affemblies at Court, and every time I was the fubject of general converfation.. They took great pleafure in tracing back many events and circumftances of my former appearance in that town; this in particular, when at the affembly, feveral charming ladies were eager to take me on their lap and clafp me in their arms: I could not help obferving to them that, being twenty-two, I had the feelings of a man, though in fize like a child. His Moft Serene Highnefs was fo good as to appoint a day for the concert, all the expences of which he defired to clear.

After having taken my leave of their Highneffes, I directed my route to Tefchen, where, being arrived, I fent to the Prince de la Tour and Taxis, that I might be permitted to pay my refpects to him. He anfwered—that he had often feen men of my

fpecies,

ſpecies, and had no curioſity to ſee any
more, except one who had travelled with
the Counteſs Humieſka, whom he had always deſired to ſee, without ever having had
it in his power. When he was told that I was
not only the very ſame he had deſired to meet
with, and that I was the bearer of letters
from the Princeſs his daughter, and the
Prince Radziwill his ſon-in-law, which
would confirm the faƈt, he ſent a carriage
for me.

After having bowed to the Prince and
all his court, I approached His Highneſs,
and told him that one of the moſt charming
ladies in the world had charged me to embrace him with all my heart. Without giving me time to finiſh my phraſe, the Prince
lifted me up in his arms, ſaying,—' 'Tis
' with great pleaſure, my little man.' Then,
having put me on the ground again, he
aſked me, ' Who had charged me with ſo
' agreeable a commiſſion ?—I immediately
delivered

delivered to him the letters of the Prince
his fon-in-law, and of the Princefs his daughter; and told him that, the day before my
fetting out from Warfaw, having waited on
the Princefs to receive her orders, fhe had
been fo kind as to embrace me, and fay,—
‘ It was on condition I would return this
‘ kifs to her papa.’—She afterwards had
enjoined me to prefs him to take a trip to
Poland, to fee a daughter who loved him
tenderly, and to whofe happinefs his prefence only was wanting; fhould he not de-
termine on it, nothing could hold her back;
but fhe would fet out immediately, not being able to live any longer without the pleafure of feeing him. During all this recital,
the Prince’s fenfibility was not equivocal;
his eyes fparkled with tears; and, after having read the letters, he embraced me again,
afked many queftions of the manner I had
parted from the Countefs Hûmiefka, of my
marriage, of what had induced me to undertake new travels; and, feeming fatisfied
with

with my anfwers, he faid, 'You muſt needs
' be fatigued, go to reſt; I will give orders
' that you want nothing. It will be proper
' for you to fpend here four or five days, to
' walk about and enjoy the benefit of the
' air.'—When I went home I faw that the
Prince's orders had preceded me; and
during four or five days I ſtaid at Tefchen,
there was nothing but feaſts and entertainments. In fine, when I took my leave of
His Highneſs, he engaged me to pay a viſit
to the Prince de Wallerſtein his fon-in-law,
who at that time refided at Honnaltheim,
his country-feat. This propoſal was too
agreeable to be refuſed.

Being arrived at Honnaltheim, I was
prefented to the Prince de Wallerſtein, by
whom, confidering the recommendation I
had from his father-in-law, I could not fail
to be kindly reċeived. But though he welcomed me with all the affability and polite-
neſs imaginable, I foon perceived that he

was

was labouring under a dark melancholy, and seemed to value life only for his extreme attachment to the Princess his daughter, then four years old. I was soon informed of the cause of this sadness, in which all his court took the greatest concern; and my astonishment ceased when I was told, that the moment which made him a father, deprived him of a charming and adored consort, for whom he had mourned ever since. She who was to complete his happiness, had plunged him into this state of apathy and insensibility, subsequent to the most violent ravings, which had alarmed his court, first for his life, and afterwards for his senses. Yet, notwithstanding this sadness, as my figure and manners seemed to amuse the young Princess, and nothing could make any impression upon him but what interested this child, the Prince did me the honour to attend my concert.

Till then, I had no reason but to applaud myself for the expedient I had taken of travelling;

velling; I had every where been seen with pleasure, and met with much civility. But nothing can be compared to the reception I found at the court of his Most Serene Highness the Margrave of Anspach, at Triersdorff; nor can I find expressions strong enough to describe the sentiments of respectful gratitude I shall always have for this amiable Prince, whose generous treatment has made the deepest impressions on my heart. 'Tis to the Mademoiselle Clairon I am indebted for it; and with the greatest pleasure do I embrace this oportunity of paying her my homage for such a favour. That distinguished actress, after having acquired so universal and so well merited a reputation, seeking only to enjoy a peaceful and easy life in the circle of a chosen society, spent every summer at Triersdorff, where she was detained by the kindness, I will venture to say, the tender friendship His Highness honoured her with. Having had the advantage of being acquainted with her at Paris in my first travels, being at supper one

evening

evening with the Princefs Galien, the Ruf-fian Ambaffadrefs, fhe faw me again with new pleafure, and was fo obliging as to pre-fent me to the Margrave. She reprefented to him, in fo affecting and lively a manner, the difference of my prefent fituation from what I had enjoyed when protected by the Countefs Humiefka, that fhe infpired this good Prince with that uncommon intereft he has fince taken in me. I had the honour to partake of his table almoft every day; after dinner I was admitted to play at fhittle-cock with Her Highnefs; and, as I was telerably fkilful at this exercife, which fuits my fize fo well, they feemed to take great pleafure in feeing me play.

I paffed fix weeks in that delightful place, amidft pleafures, entertainments, and that friendly protection which is fo flatter-ing when it comes from the great. I can-not remember without feeling the utmoft fenfe of endlefs gratitude, with what good-

nature

nature their Highneſſes offered to take care
of my daughter; I do not ceaſe to praiſe
the bleſſed day that procured me ſo illuſ-
trious a benefactor, when I recollect how
earneſt this good Prince was to calm my inquietudes for the fate of this child; and
that on perceiving her mother's grief to part
with an only child, he deigned to addreſs
me with theſe remarkable words, which are
ſtill echoed to the bottom of my heart:—
' My friend, it is not only a Prince's word
' I give you to take care of' your child, re-
' ceive that of an honeſt man, and be aſ-
' ſured that I will provide for her.'—O! my
daughter, I ſhall leave you no inheritance;
reduced inceſſantly to ſtruggle with fortune,
your father is compelled to ſeek for every
poſſible means of providing for his ſubſiſt-
ence; but here he bequeaths you to the ſa-
cred word of a magnanimous Prince, and,
ſhould you know how to value ſo great a
favour, your happineſs muſt neceſſarily be
the conſequence.

Some

Some days after we prepared to fet out, and on taking our leave, Her Highnefs deigned to give us repeated affurances of the fate of our child. I could not make any other return but my tears, for fo many tokens of beneficence, and it was with the bittereft regret I tore myfelf from a place which I had fo much reafon to be partial to,—which every thing has contributed to render interefting to me.

On leaving Trierfdorff, my only care was to haften my journey, that I might reach England as foon as poffible. I have already obferved that his Excellency Sir Robert Murry Keith, had prevailed upon me to take this rout, by having affured me a thoufand times that I could not fail of making a brilliant fortune, in a country were generofity and greatnefs of foul, are reckoned among the characteriftic virtues of the nation.

Therefore,

Therefore, after having paſſed rapidly through, Franckfort, Mayence, and Manheim, I went to Straſburg, where I had the honour to give a concert, under the protection of the Princeſs Chriſtiana, to whom I alſo had the honour to preſent a letter of recommendation from the Electoreſs of Bavaria her ſiſter, who politely engaged me to ſpend ſeveral evenings at her court. The night before my departure, I received from her hands a handſome gold box, of three colours, which ſhe had ordered to be made for me, and which cruel neceſſity has compelled me to didſoſe of during my reſidence in London.

I afterwards directed my courſe to Bruſſels, where I had the honour to be preſented to the governor and his lady of the Low Countries; all the nobility welcomed me with much kindneſs; I was even permitted to preſide at a concert in an elegant room fitted up for their aſſemblies, of which they

defrayed

defrayed the expences. Meeting with some
unexpected disappointments, this concert
did not answer my expectations. But the
generous public by no means imputed the
blame to me, and I had every reason to be
satisfied with their proceedings. I remained
at Bruffells during two months, then I em-
barked for Oftend.

I had never been at sea, nor ever beheld
this proud element. Judge then with what
amazement and admiration I contemplated
so tremendous a spectacle, such a depth and
extent of boisterous waters, upon which I
was soon to expose my own life, and what
I held deareft in the world. I confidered
the main as likely to be my grave; and my
apprehenfions were very nearly realized.
During a paffage of four days we were con-
tinually toffed in ftorms, our mafts broke,
our fails were carried away; and if to my
own fituation is added that which I fuffered
for the ftate of my wife, who was afflicted
with great ficknefs and fpitting of blood,
which nothing could ftop; it may eafily be

conceived

conceived the fatisfaction I felt on our getting out of the packet. We landed at Mar-
gate, the 20th of March, 1782, and a few
days after fet out for London, where we arrived without any other accident.

We had brought with us a number of
recommendatory letters to many of the firft
nobility. I immediately made ufe of thofe
directed to their Graces the Duke and
Duchefs of Devonfhire ; and though I had
every where heard them praifed for their
politenefs, their affability, their defire of
obliging, yet I foon learnt by myfelf that
true merit is always fuperior to the higheft
renown. This illuftrious couple received
me moft gracioufly, and condefcended to
fay :—that having heard of my misfurtunes,
they defired I would have recourfe to them
if I wanted any thing.—The Duchefs afterwards afked me many queftions, with that
affability and feeling concern, which, far
from denoting an eager curiofity, only wait
for anfwers that may give occafion to beftow favours. In effect, having been informed

formed that I was not lodged conveniently, and that for want of speaking the language, I could hardly provide for my necessaries, she immediately gave orders to procure me a comfortable lodging at her own expence; this we held some months. The very next day, Her Grace having been informed that my wife was ill, sent Dr. Walker to attend her; and I esteem this not the smallest favour of the Duchess to have procured me the acquaintance of so respectable a gentleman, whose friendship to me has not ceased during my stay in England, bestowing upon me and my family, his cares and remedies with generosity, in a manner that puts it entirely out of my power to acknowledge what I feel.

His first visit was pleasant enough. The Duchess had not informed him of the species of man whose wife she desired him to attend; coming into the apartment he took me for a child. Being near his patient's

bed,

bed, he was taken up with aſking her queſ-
tions, and I, on my part, with thanking
him, recommending the care of my wife;
and as the tone of my voice is much above
my ſtature, ſo he was at a loſs to conceive
from whence came the ſpeech that was directed to him.   My wife perceiving his
embaraſſment, told him who I was.

· Going to take my leave of the Ducheſs,
I was preſented to Lady Spencer, who was
pleaſed to appoint a day to receive me at
her houſe.   And there I had the happineſs
of ſeeing his Royal Highneſs the Prince of
Wales, to whom my Lady graciouſly preſented me; and the Prince received me
with his uſual affability, which gains him
univerſal eſteem.

Soon after my arrival in London, there
appeared a ſtupendous giant; he was eight
feet four inches high; was well proportioned,
had a pleaſing countenance, and what is not

common

common in men of his fize, his ftrength
adequate to his bulk, He was then two
and twenty years of age; many perfons
wifhed to fee us in company, particularly
the Duke and Duchefs of Devonfhire, my
worthy protectors, who with Lady Spencer,
propofing a day to fee the giant, I offered
to accompany them that they might view fo
great a contraft as his great, and my little
ftature, muft naturully afford them. I went,
and I believe we were equally aftonifhed.
The giant remained fometime mute. Then
ftooping very low he offered me his hand,
which I am fure would have inclofed a
dozen like mine. He paid me a genteel
compliment, and drew me near to him,
that the difference of our fize might ftrike
the fpectators the better: the top of my
head fcarce reached his knee.

About this time I was vifited by His
Royal Highnefs the Duke of Gloucefter, at
whofe door I had called as foon as I arrived,
to deliver a letter which His Highnefs the
Margrave

Margrave of Anfpach had favoured me with
for him.   But as I had not been fortunate
enough to meet him, he thought proper to
furprize me with a vifit incognito: but
Mr. Cramer, the firft violin, engaged at his
Majefty's concert, who having come to fee
me, met with his Royal Highnefs, and thus
preventing his remaining any longer incognito, gave him an opportunity of affuring
me I might depend he would do all in his
power to oblige me.   From that time this
amiable prince has not ceafed to favour me
with proofs of his protection.   Unhappily
for me, the epoch of his Royal Highnefs's
travels was fixed, and I felt the mortifica-
tion of feeing him fet out foon after my
arrival.

The Duchefs of Devonfhire, as well as
her whole family, ftill continued to take the
moft lively intereft in all that related to me,
well knowing that my fituation was beneath my birth, education, and fentiments;
fhe recommended me to all her acquaintance.

ance. I ought to diftinguifh in the number
the Countefs of Egremont, fince it is to her
I owe the obligation of being prefented to
their Majefties. Her Ladyfhip having been
informed that I was fpoken of at Court,
ftuffed one of my fhoes with cotton, and
fent it to the queen; this exciting their curiofity, their Majefties condefcended to appoint a day for me to attend them.

It was on the 23d of May, 1782, that
my Lady Egremout was fo kind as to take
me to her Majefty. The King and all the
Royal Family were prefent. His Majefty
condefcended to bid me fit down, and afked
me many queftions. H. R. H. the Prince
of Wales often interrupted the converfation
by witty and agreeable fallies; and the young
Princes and Princeffes recovering from the
firft aftonifhment I had caufed them, entered with me into the familiarities which
characterizes youth. In fine, I had the
honour to ftay four hours with their Ma-

jefties;

jefties; and having ufed all my efforts to pleafe them, I enjoyed the fatisfaction of feeing that, in fome refpect, I had not failed in my aim.

These exertions, however, were near being fatal to me; I came home with a fever, and the very next day fell dangeroufly ill. His Majefty did me the favour to fend his phyfician, Sir Richard Jebb, by whofe care, together with that of our good friend Dr. Walker, I recovered in a fortnight.

The public have fpoken very freely with regard to that vifit; it has been mentioned in fome news-papers, that I received from Their Majefties a confiderable fum of money; but it is with this report as with many others which are founded on conjectures only. If it had the leaft foundation in truth, I would not have omitted any of its particulars; as I confider it my duty to declare

all

all the favours I have been indulged with.
The fact is, that His Majesty vouchsafed to
treat me as a Pólish gentleman; and though
it is an honour to receive favours from a
King, yet these marks of royal condescend-
ance obliterated every idea of interest.

But alas! we must suppress the dictates
of self-love, when the matter in question is
to provide for the subsistence of those who
are dearest to us; it was soon necessary that
this last consideration should prevail with
me above all others. Besides, though it
were possible to have always recourse to
generous benefactors, do we not experience
more painful, more humiliating sentiments,
in incessantly importuning them, than if by
some other means we could succeed in pro-
curing ourselves a decent maintenance?

Such were the reflections which arose
in my mind, from my own situation, and
which met with the approbation of those to

whom

whom I communicated them. They advised me to give concerts; afterwards they prevailed upon me to make an exhibition of myfelf, and the preffure of want and the call of nature, had ftifled in my heart all that feemed fhocking to me in fuch an expedient.

The firft concert I gave was at Carlifle Houfe, Soho. My Lady Egremont always anxious for my welfare, was frightened at the expence it occafioned me, and which actually amounted to eighty guineas; but I was amply indemnified, the affembly being both brilliant and numerous; and if that enthufiafm had continued, fome concerts given now and then would have been fufficient to fet me above mediocrity: this, however, did not happen; for having attempted a few weeks after to give another at the fame place, I fcarcely cleared my expences; half the nobility were gone to the country, the others were departing, and I

was

was obliged to think of new means of
fupport.

At the beginning of the winter following I went to Bath, where I met with moft
of my protectors. At my return to London, refpect and gratitude led me to the
door of the Duchefs of Devonfhire, but
notwithftanding many attempts, it was impoffible for me to obtain admittance. I was
afraid I had incurred her Grace's difplea-
fure; when Lady Clermont affured me that
this powerful protectrefs ftill entertained the
fame fentiments for me, and I fhould foon
be convinced of it.

This converfation recalled to my mind
what feveral Lords, who about fix months
before met at my apartment, made me
hope for. The defign was to open a fubfcription, at the head of which the moft illuftrious of my protectors would be put, to
fecure me an eafy and decent maintenance

for

for the remainder of my days. They had come fo 'often to queftion me upon this fubjeft, and the concern they feemed to have for me was fo evident, that for a while I ventured to flatter myfelf that this projeft would take place; but it failed, and I faw myfelf deprived of profitable and honourable fupport.

I was then compelled to try fome other plan, as the vifits I received would by no means fupport the expences. I therefore determined to renew my concerts, the profits arifing gave me a temporal relief; and I fet out for Ireland in the month of April, 1783. But forefeeing this trip would be longer than I expefted, I ftopped at Briftol, intending to leave it in a week, but remained there two months, and I have no reafon to complain: for though I did not intend to ftay fo long, I enjoyed every fatisfaction I could wifh; which I attribute in part to the marks of friendfhip fhewn

me

me by Mr. Humberry, and the humane difpofitions of the inhabitants. I have fince renewed my vifit to this truly opulent city, and was honoured with many diftinguifhed teftimonies of the benevolence of its inhabitants, as elevated in fentiment as their city in fplendour.——From thence I went to Chefter, where the civilities and kindnefs I met with detained me feven weeks.

It was during my ftay there, I got acquainted with one of thofe men, who, having received of nature, wit and good appearance, think themfelves exempt from being principled with honour and uprightnefs, and who, compelled through their want of conduct to leave their own country, eftablifh their refources in foreign lands, upon the credulity and good faith of thofe whom they find means to infpire with confidence. This man affumed the name of Marquis de Montpellier, and for a while was very cautious not to come to my apartments but among great folks, with whom

he

he ſtrove to act an officious part, in order to give me a good opinion of his connections. Nor did he fail in his deſign; as he had artfully perſuaded me that he entertained intimacy with the firſt nobility of Ireland,—that, if he would attempt it, nothing could be ſo eaſy for him as to procure me there a ſubſcription of two thouſand five hundred guineas,—that for this purpoſe he had only to ſet out before me, to ſecure an houſe, and announce my coming, in order to prepare their minds for my reception, ſo that I could not help giving credit to all the chimeras he lulled me with. Thus the pretended Marquis ſet out, having my full powers; and I followed him in a fortnight after. We had a fortunate paſſage, and as Lady Clermont had condeſcended to give me a letter for the maſter of the packet, I had much reaſon to be pleaſed with the attentions and care of the captain and all his crew, who, notwithſtanding my entreaties, however preſſing I was, would not accept even the leaſt gratification for their trouble. On my arrival

rival in Dublin I hoped to have found a
houfe ready for me; but was extremely furprized at meeting my fellow in an inn near
the port, where he had announced me for
a great Lord, and, thanks to his provident
cares, I fared very daintly, not yet perceiving that I was his dupe. Nay, it was not
till a fortnight after, that being informed by
refpectable perfons, both of the pretended
Marquis's character, and the harm that
fuch an acquaintance would do me, I had
wifdom enough to get rid of this parafite,
by giving him money to crofs the fea again.

When I fet out from London, my protectors had been fo attentive as to fupply
me with letters of recommendation, as well
to His Grace the Lord Lieutenant, as to the
chief Lords and moft of the diftinguifhed
Ladies in Ireland. My Lord Viceroy fent
or me to his Court, on an affembly-day, and
to judge by my reception, I afforded them
much pleafure. Some time afer he was

fucceeded

fucceeded by His Grace the Duke of Rutland, under whofe patronage and that of the Duchefs, I had the honour to give the Irifh nobility a concert and ball at the Rotunda, in May, 1784. The affembly was extremely brilliant; Her Grace the Vice Reine was the principal ornament.

His Grace the Duke of Leinfter, on this occafion gave me a gracious reception. His greatnefs of foul, his bounty, are written with indelible charaƈters in the hearts of many unhappy creatures, whom he relieves during the feverity of the winter, both in town and his country-feats, in a manner as judicious as charitable. I myfelf faw an aƈt of humanity, which 1 am in duty bound to relate. As he paffed on horfeback through Dame-ftreet, an unlucky fervant, whofe foot had flipt as he was getting behind a coach, fell between the hind wheel and the body. Happily for the man, the Duke at that infant, was near the coach; he

alights,

alights, and flying to the horfes, ftops them, and takes out the poor fellow, whom one turn more of the wheel would have crufhed to death.

After remaining near two years in Ireland, much longer than I intended, in compliance to feveral preffing intreaties, I at length fet out, and rapidly travelling through Liverpool, Manchefter and Birmingham, repaired to Oxford, where I made a confiderable ftay.

One day a gentleman came and defired me to go and fpend the evening at about eight or nine miles diftance. He would not tell the place, but affured me that a carriage fhould take me thither, and I fhould not repent my vifit. I complied with his requeft; and how great was my furprize, when I found myfelf conveyed to the magnificent palace at Blenheim, where Their Graces the Duke and Duchefs of Marl-

borough

borough welcomed me in the moſt affable manner. The Ducheſs herſelf vouchſafed to ſhew the apartments, and point out all the curious pieces they contain. I. played upon the guitar.

At length I returned to London in March, 1786, after about three years abſence. I met there with the Grand General of Lithuania, the Count Oginſki, who had ſhewn me ſo much kindneſs during my ſtay at Paris. He ſeemed to take much pleaſure in ſeeing me again, and promiſed to aſſiſt me on all occaſions with his name and credit.

This was a moſt favourable opportunity for me to perform another concert under the inſpection of this nobleman, ſo approved for talents of every kind, who had deigned to teach me the firſt elements of muſic. The day appointed was the 30th of June. His Royal Highneſs the Prince of Wales promiſed promifed to be prefent. He had at dinner with him on that day, His Highnefs the Prince de Mecklenburgh, and wifhing to fhew me to this Prince, he fent his carriage for me. I found Their Highneffes at table, with whom I fat down a full hour, and from thence fet out for the concert. Though it was tolerably well performed, and before a chofen affembly, yet I fhould have fuffered a lofs, if the generous Count Oginfki had not paid Mr. Gallini all the charges of it.

About that time I was informed that His Grace the Duke of Marlborough wifhed to have one of my fhoes, to place it in his cabinet among other rarities: I had had too much reafon to be flattered with this nobleman's affability not to fend him a pair of them immediately, to which I joined the only pair of boots I had made for me, which I brought from Poland: His Grace was very well pleafed with this mark of attention.

It

It was about this time in agitation to give the public an hiftory of my life. Many perfons of quality, as well as naturalifts, preffed me to undertake it; and I received a number of fubfcriptions; His Royal Highnefs the Prince of Wales was gracioufly pleafed to be at the head of the fubfcribers. Therefore I ought only to mind this tafk, and do my beft endeavours to render fuch work, according to the very fmall abilities I had, worthy the patronage of fo many perfons, who condefcended to intereft themfelves for me. But let me be permitted to pafs over in filence all the difficulties and croffes I met with, in an undertaking which required many recollections, and more time than was imagined at firft. I will only fay, and that with the utmoft gratitude, that I could never have brought it about, without the bounty of the Princefs Lubomirfka, who deigned to enter into the minuteft detail of my fituation, and on feeing I was expofed to vexations from ill-natured creditors, ready to profecute me, afked for an account of my debts. I can never forget fuch an act of beneficence, fince, by reftoring me to tranquility, it has put it in my power to finifh this performance.

I had long intended to travel through Scotland : a refpectable lady to whom I was under great obligations when at Norwich, gave me feveral letters of recommendation; fhe even procured me fome from Sir W. Jeringham, a Scotch Baronet, then refiding in England; and from my Lord Rofberry : furnifhed with thefe, I fet out. When at Edinburgh I paid my refpects to the Dumfrier family, and having delivered a letter of recommendation, was really made happy by the moft gracious and cordial reception. This illuftrious family gave me an immediate proof of their eagernefs to ferve me by prefiding at a public breakfaft which lafted part of the day. The company was brilliant and numerous, and J had the
happinefs

happineſs to attract the particular attention
of my viſitors, and they ſeemed much
pleaſed at my playing on the guitar.
This gala terminated with an elegant ball,
which procured me two advantages, that of
a conſiderable ſum, and that of forming an
acquaintance with the moſt reſpectable perſons in this city.—I then paſſed ſome weeks
in Glaſgow, and was perfectly well received.

Scotland is not equal to England in
the richneſs of ſoil or beauty of ſituation,
and the winter much ſeverer; but the can-
dour, probity, frankneſs and affability of this
truly amiable and benevolent nation, would
render even a deſart delightful.—My little
heart glows with ſentiments of gratitude,
when I reflect on the gracious reception I
met with and the advantages accruing there-
from.   O, humane and benevolent people!
Nothing but the utmoſt malice of fortune
ſhall prevent me from executing a project

refolved on at the moment of my parting with you,---that is, to return again.

I am now bound for France; but alas, how different my fituation from the time when I went protected by my benefactrefs, Countefs Humiefka. I refolved to ftay at fome town with a view to defray the expences of fo long and tedious a journey; I fucceeded pretty well at York, Bath, and fome other places upon my road, where I received both pleafure and profit, as I had done before, in feveral parts of this kingdom.

I difembarked at Boulogna, foon in the fpring, 1790, and fucceeded in forming an acquaintance with fome amatures of mufic; who, amongft many other favours, procured me a concert, and very politely performed themfelves to fave my expences. I then fet out for L'Ifle, in Flanders, but made no ftay; it was juft after the revolu-

tion,

tion, and that extraordinary event engrossed all their attention. I thought I might succeed better in going to Paris; I arrived in June the same year; and had once more the honour to see many noblemen, who, thirty years ago, when I was with the Countess, honoured me with their attention, and now renewed their civilities. The Marquis of D'Almazasque interested himself in my behalf, and presented me to Monsieur the present King's (Louis XVI.) brother, who received me with the same transcending condescension as his Britannic Majesty had done some years ago.

I then endeavoured to give a concert, which by no means answered my expectation, though seconded by a lady of distinguished rank, and merit; and on mature reflection, I clearly perceived that all Paris, the ladies not excepted, were absorbed in contemplating their new form of Constitution, and that this grand object re-

moving

moving every other idea, I had little to expect from the accustomed urbanity of the French nobility, and my purse being very low, this intervention must prove a total eclipse. If I remained much longer here, I said to myself, I swim against the stream; and I resolved to go to Cherburg, which is the nearest French port to Guernsey, where I wished to go; and having made a bargain, dear enough, with the master of a Smack, I went on board the 29th of April, 1791, and meeting with bad weather, I did not arrive till the 3d of May at night; and though only 54 miles distant, many in my place would enumerate the eminent dangers they had experienced in this voyage---I shall content myself by just saying, I was not sorry when I got on shore---no other loss was sustained than a fowl, who finding himself too closely pent up in the hold, jumped over board to be more at liberty. I had not room to lie down in this vessel, though only three passengers on board; however, I

was

was not sea sick, and indeed seldom am, at sea. Our vessel was worked by Captains, but never a sailor. It was called the *Little St. John*, but the inhabitants of Guernsey changed its name, and called it a *Hen-coop*, which was by far a more proper appellation.

When I arrived, I delivered my letters of recommendation addressed to some of the principal inhabitants. I remained here two months; and, gave a ball; the number of ladies who attended made a genteel appearance.

This island, 21 miles in circumference, is charming; the country pleasant and fruitful; for in so small a compass they make yearly two hundred and fifty barrels of cyder; its inhabitants amount to near two thousand. The air is good, the water excellent, and trade flourishing; and there was a citadel just finished, besides other forts

with

with batteries of cannon, furrounding this
ifland, though well fortified by nature.

The Governor gave me a genteel invitation on St. George's day, and I had the
honour to dine with him and feveral officers of the Garrifon, who were invited to
celebrate the King's birth-day. He fhewed
me every attention, and the reft of the gentlemen were by no means deficient.

The favourite reception I met with
from the inhabitants of Guernfey, and the
pains they took to ferve me, particularly
thofe to whom I was recommended, claims
my fincere and moft refpectful acknow-
ledgements, and much I efteem myfelf
indebted to them.

I failed from thence in June, but in a
larger veffel; and on my return to England
vifited fome towns where I had not been
before; efpecially Hereford, where I ftopped

some time, and gave a ball and concert, which was attended by the moſt diſtinguiſhed families of the town and neighbourhood, by whom I was loaded with kindneſs, and in a more peculiar manner by the worthy family of Mr. Cam.

From Hereford I came to Birmingham, where I met with a reception equally kind; here through the intereſt of Mr. Biſſet, ſecretary and treaſurer to the Debating Society, I was made a member of the ſame, and honoured with a ſilver medal, ſuch as that Mr. Beddoes, the preſident at that time, was the only gentleman decorated with, and which I ſhall carefully keep as a token of my eternal gratitude. Some time after I was invited to go to Henley, to attend the eſtabliſhment and conſecration of a new Free-maſon lodge, where the Free-maſons of the neighbouring towns had been invited. When the ceremony was over, we repaired to a hall which had been temporally built

for

for the celebration of the feaſt, and which
was like to be overturned by the croud;
but as ſoon as I made my appearance at
the door, the people were ſo aſtoniſhed to
ſee me, ·that immediately tranquility was
reſtored, and we dined quietly.

I propoſe going to Ireland for the ſame
reaſon, and from thence to Scotland; induced by my own inclination and the preſſing invitation of many reſpectable perſons,
when I left them. ·

I am come at laſt to a concluſion of the
·principal events of my life: I have deſcribed, as much as in my power, my ad-
ventures, my ſentiments, the unfolding of my
intellectual faculties,—have gone back to
the time of each event. On examining my
heart, I have ſtill found in it the ſame ſentiments, the ſame ſource from whence aroſe
my pleaſures, my errors and misfortunes,—
and following this current, have diſcovered
a very

a very comfortable truth:—that a man of feeling never regrets thofe actions which originate from tendernefs of fentiment, when unaccompanied by felf-reproach.—After having fpoken of what I have done and thought, may I be permitted to fix my reader's attention for a mo-ment upon my whole life, and my prefent fituation.

I have fpent my youth in pleafures and opulence. At this epoch, when nature claims her rights, I gave way, and perhaps might have been loft---reflection and good advice have had the power to draw me from a licentious life, and I eafily fubdued thofe pleafures that enfnared me: but it was not fo when my inclinations were fixed on a virtuous object. I forgot in one mo-ment what I owed to my benefactrefs, to myfelf, to confiftency; it feemed that love would not admit any other fentiment in my heart; I became ungrateful; I left with-

out

out regret a houfe, which, fome time before, I could not have given up but on feeling a mortal grief; at laft, I united myfelf to her for whom I had facrificed all, and I was at the height of my wifhes. His Majefty, the King of Poland, vouchfafed to favour me with one hundred and twenty ducats annuity. On finding this to be infufficient, my friends prevailed upon me to travel; I have been every where kindly received, and agreeably entertained,—every where loaded with prefents; but all is fwallowed up by the confiderable expences which a long refidence in towns required.

At length I arrived in England: Here I excite a kind of enthufiafm; a calculation is immediately formed on the generofity, of fome particular benefactors, without confidering the enormous expences unavoidable in that fort of life I was obliged to lead. It is reported that I have laid out fix thoufand pounds in the funds: this report

port reaches my own country, it gets ground there; hence it is concluded, I want the King's favours no longer, and my annuity is cut off;---in that very moment, when Lady Egremont deigns openly to protect a fubfcription, with a view to procure me a fubfiftence,—when the Princefs Lubomirfka, affected at my diftrefs, clears my debts.

Behold me now by the vague and malicious report of an imaginary fortune deprived of a real refource, and plunged in poverty and diftrefs.

Thefe are paft evils, but what will be my future lot, heaven only knows.   Am I to remain the fport of cruel fortune, and the flave of the monent? What do I fay? Were I willing to fubmit to this humiliating idea, what hope can arife of an honeft eftablifhment for my wife and children?— Old age comes faft upon me; when gone, what will become of my little ones and

their

their tender mother; to whom can ſhe fly for ſuccour? Am I then doomed in the decline of life, to miſery and wretch-edneſs, deprived of every ſoothing hope for thoſe I cheriſh? Behold the cruel pangs of a huſband and father; were I upon a footing with other mortals, I might, like them, have ſupported myſelf and family, by honeſt induſtry: but my ſize excludes me irrevocably from the common circle of ſo-ciety.—There are many perſons who ſeem to pay no regard, nor even to conſider me as a man, and an honeſt man, endued with the moſt tender ſenſibility,—how painful a reflection!

To you I addreſs myſelf, O Britons! Bleſt nation, renowned for generoſity, be-nevolence and humanity; the admiration of the world!—If I ſink under my misfor-tunes, I earneſtly recommend to you my wife and children, your fellow citizens by birth, honoured in the title of countrymen.

Compelled

Compelled by my unhappy pofition, ftill to wander, God knows where: may his provi-dence be my guide. But in whatever country or climate fate directs me, I will ever have prefent---yes, I will precioufly hoard up in my memory, and retain in the inmoft recefles of my foul, the indelible fentiments of love and gratitude that your benevolence has juftly impreffed.—May the fupreme Being fhelter this country from inteftine troubles; and may it ever flourifh in peace and plenty.

FINIS.

www.ingramcontent.com/pod-product-compliance
Lightning Source LLC
Chambersburg PA
CBHW020013030726
47500CB00002B/561